STOLEN BY THE BRATVA

AVA GRAY

ALSO BY AVA GRAY

When We Meet Again

The Rules We Break

Secret Baby with my Boss's Brother

Frosty Beginnings

Silver Fox Billionaire

Taken by the Major

Daddy's Unexpected Gift

Off Limits

Playing with Trouble Series:

Chasing What's Mine

Claiming What's Mine

Protecting What's Mine

Saving What's Mine

The Beckett Billionaires Series:

Love to Hate You

Just Another Chance

Standalone's:

Ruthless Love

The Best Friend Affair

. . .

PARANORMAL ROMANCE

Maple Lake Shifters Series:

Omega Vanished

Omega Exiled

Omega Coveted

Omega Bonded

Everton Falls Mated Love Series:

The Alpha's Mate

The Wolf's Wild Mate

Saving His Mate

Fighting For His Mate

Dragons of Las Vegas Series:

Thin Ice

Silver Lining

A Spark in the Dark

Fire & Ice

Dragons of Las Vegas Boxed Set (The Complete Series)

Standalone's:

Fiery Kiss

Wild Fate

BLURB

A steamy, twisted dark romance filled with spice and hotness!

MILA

My father always says I'm too fat to be desirable.

His solution? Marry me off to the enemy...

But instead of falling for my fiancé, I discover my attraction to Aleksei Valkov.

I'm supposed to marry his cousin, but I can't ignore my feelings for dangerous, stubborn and seductive Aleksei.

But when my past threatens our happy ending, I quickly realize more than just my marriage is at stake.

It's my life, too.

ALEKSEI

I was never meant to get so obsessed with my cousin's bride-to-be.

But she's a threat, and I have no other option than to kidnap her to keep my Bratva safe.

Except Mila Kastava clearly isn't the enemy here .

Her family is.

So would it really be so bad if I let temptation in with the gorgeous, curvy bombshell who I can trick into giving me her V-card?

I don't think I can resist a little off-limits treat like Mila.

STOLEN BY THE BRATVA **is a full-length, standalone spicy mafia romance. One-click for an older billionaire hero, and a curvy virgin heroine! Kidnapping included for your pleasure ;)**

1

ALEK

The man cried out as Ivan held him back. Blood, sweat, and tears coated the spy's shirt. They mixed and merged as he sobbed and begged for mercy.

Mercy? That wasn't in the cards for him. If anyone thought they could spy on the Valkov territory and get away with it, they had another thing coming.

"Please, I wasn't here to look around," the idiot insisted through his tears. Losing two of his fingers had to hurt, but I kept my knife poised and ready to remove a lot more. Whatever it took to get him talking. I refused to go easy on this spy.

The Rossini Family were always looking for ways to get to us, but they would learn their lesson one way or another. No one messed with the Valkov Bratva.

"Aleksei." My cousin's mocking tone slurred as he entered the warehouse. As soon as Ivan and I captured this Rossini spy lurking outside —taking fucking pictures through the windows—we called Andrey and let him know what we were up to with this development. Andrey was my superior in theory only. If my cousin actually gave a shit and acted like the heir to the Bratva, I would have held a semblance of respect for him. But he didn't care. He could barely walk into this windowless room of the basement, used strictly for dealing with enemies and fools. Calling Andrey here was nothing more than a polite gesture. His arrival wouldn't change anything. I couldn't remember the last time my cousin had cared about hearing intel from a spy.

He tsked, approaching me and Ivan. Ivan glanced at me, a wary, skeptical lift of his brows as he, too, wondered why Andrey had bothered. Most times, he ignored business matters and let everything go to voicemails. Maybe he'd get off his lazy ass and reply with a vague text.

I kept my blade ready even though I almost got the sense that Andrey would, for once, involve himself here. My cousin disliked ever getting his hands dirty. He couldn't possibly want to handle the torture personally.

"What's the meaning of this?" he asked, frowning at the spy we'd captured, then glancing at his watch.

What? What the fuck? "I called and informed you of the spy trying to get a way into our warehouse." *Just how fucking drunk are you if you can't remember a call from ten minutes ago?*

"A *spy?*" Andrey smirked, walking in a slow circle around us.

Ivan didn't release the Italian. If anything, my brother held the spy tighter with the bloody rope tugging his neck tight. I remained tense, holding my blade and waiting for my cousin to leave. Treating him like he was in charge was a joke. His father, the bratva's Pakhan, was no better.

"He's not a spy," Andrey said dismissively, almost bored.

"He was outside trying to take pictures of our product," Ivan argued evenly.

"No, I wasn't. It's a misunderstanding," the Italian rushed to add. "Just an accident."

"Bullshit," I spat, stepping closer with my knife. My shoes crunched over his phone. I'd already shattered the device on the concrete floor.

"Ah, just let him go. We don't need to bother with this." Andrey waved at the door, but Ivan didn't let the man go. I didn't back up either. "He's not worth your time."

"We can't let him go. He was spying." I narrowed my eyes at my cousin, wondering how he could be so deluded. If we let this man go, he'd tell his Mafia brothers about how lax the bratva had become.

"He didn't see anything." Andrey shrugged. "It's not like the Rossinis are a threat anymore."

"They are *all* threats," I argued.

"Not the Rossinis," Andrey retorted. "They're nothing now, not after losing so many with all their infighting."

It didn't matter if the Rossinis were strong or weak. They were our rivals, and we couldn't go easy on them.

"This is what you pulled me away from the whores for?" Andrey scoffed, shaking his head. "Just let him go. Give him a warning if you want." He shrugged. "I don't care. I just want to get back to the pussies waiting for me in my bed."

His priorities were shit. Andrey—and his father—cared more about drinking and fucking the whores. But letting this Italian go with a goddamn warning was asking for trouble.

"It's foolhardy to release him," Ivan warned in a firm tone. Not many messed with my brother when he spoke like that, but Andrey was oblivious, smirking at him.

"We can't be *this* sloppy," I argued.

Andrey shook his head. "It's not being sloppy. It's letting stupid shit that doesn't matter go."

I failed to see how he saw a spy as *stupid shit* that should be ignored. I'd never held Andrey or Pavel in high esteem, but they were the head of the family. Their word was law. More and more, though, I wondered if they'd bring the whole bratva to ruin with their lousy leadership.

"This isn't something to just let go," Ivan protested. "Too many spies are waiting to sneak in. Our rivals will take advantage of any information they can get about our business."

He laughed it off. Each chuckle grated on my nerves.

"Take advantage of *us*? The Valkov Bratva is too powerful," Andrey bragged.

"Was. We *were* powerful," I replied hotly. Ever since my father died in a turf war, the bratva had been declining in influence. I always thought my father did the Pakhan's work for him, and with his death, the leadership crumbled.

"We still are. We're the most powerful crime organization in New York," Andrey drawled, like I was the idiot here.

"No." I shook my head. "Not anymore. It seems like the Ortez Cartel reigns."

"We're not declining," Andrey said, not touching on my comment about the cartel. I doubted he could lie about their influence.

"And once we align with the Kastava Family, all will be well." He smoothed down his suit jacket, pompous as ever. "Uniting with the Kastavas will bring strength in numbers with more forces."

I furrowed my brow, hating that he would talk about this in front of a spy. "Those are just rumors. No alliance will form between the Valkovs and Kastavas."

Pavel had mentioned talking with Sergei Kastava and entering negotiations with him, but nothing had happened from those chats yet. Still, speaking about this union in front of the Italian was careless.

"I'm not sure I'd trust the Kastavas, anyway."

Andrey sneered. "That's not your call to make."

"The Kastavas have a long history of lying," Ivan added.

"It's already a done deal." Andrey shoved one hand in his pocket, tumbling his keys with his fingers in an annoying jingle. "I'm marrying the eldest daughter, Mila Kastava. Our marriage will solidify and celebrate the alliance that will pave the way for our critical shipment."

Now the spy really would have to die. I couldn't believe my cousin would speak about our biggest shipment to date. The sheer number of arms and contraband we were supposed to receive would be a boon in revenue. Mentioning it in front of this Rossini had just guaranteed his death.

"Father demanded this marriage happen to go with the agreement. The Kastavas will get a portion of our arms, and they will grant us use of their Colver docks."

Andrey wasn't talking out of his ass. We'd been hoping to take over or secure the Colver docks for decades. With so much of our business happening with transportation of goods and illegal product, we needed a better location to ship and receive. Those docks were in a prime location, not so easily accessible to the cops.

"And since my wedding will be here sooner than later," Andrey said, smiling smugly at us both, "all the more reason to enjoy the whores at home while I can." He backpedaled, chuckling. "Not that I won't be able to when I've got Mila for a wife. I've heard she's heavier than I care for, but…" He shrugged. "My mistresses can take care of me just as well."

Ivan and I shared a glance. Affairs and sleeping with mistresses were common practice in the bratva. We weren't judging him, not for that. But as he backed away, indifferent and uninterested in this spy here, we could judge him for being a pathetic leader.

"Don't call me and bother me with petty shit like this." Andrey flung his hand to the air, like shooing away this incident. "Let the man go, and don't interfere with my plans for the night. Think you can handle that?"

He didn't wait for us to reply. After pushing the door open and letting it slam shut, he washed his hands of the incident.

"Why'd we even fucking call him?" Ivan growled.

"Protocol," I reminded him. "Or it *used* to be protocol to have someone from the top be involved with these things." Not since my father had been alive and operating under Pavel's orders had anyone done things right. Protocol was an excuse of the past. Rules and expectations were forgotten and ignored.

The spy cleared his throat, pointing at the rope. "I–I–I understand. Your warning is clear. I won't come around here anymore."

I raised my knife again. His groveling irritated me, but my cousin's news pissed me off more.

"No," the Italian cried out as I approached. "He said to just warn me. To let me go." He lifted his shaking, bloody hand, minus two fingers. "You've warned me."

Ivan rolled his eyes and held the man secure. Without giving the fucker another chance to whine and beg, I sliced my blade across his neck. My brother kept him upright for a moment more. Then, as the blood puddled at our feet, he dropped the spy like the worthless sack of dead meat he was.

Unbothered by the kill and agreeing with my decision to disobey

Andrey, Ivan stepped away and began to wipe the blood from his hands. "Aligning with the Kastavas will be a mistake."

I nodded, crouching to wipe my blade on the dead spy's pants. "It will be. I understand how an agreement like that could be beneficial." Selling arms was the nature of our business. Obtaining rights to the Colver dock would be an advantage. But with the Kastavas? I had a bad feeling about this. My gut told me not to trust them. Like Andrey said, it wasn't my choice to make. Pavel had ruled with shitty decisions for a decade now, and Ivan and I, along with our three brothers, could do nothing but follow along.

"But not with them. Not the Kastavas," I said as I stood.

He shook his head, snapping his fingers for a couple of soldiers to start cleaning up the mess the spy had made. They'd dispose of his body.

Instead of being rewarded for keeping the bratva on top of their enemies and catching a spy, we had been chastised and dismissed.

"I don't like this shift," I told Ivan as we headed out of the warehouse. "Pavel doesn't know what the fuck he's doing, suggesting an alliance with Kastava."

"He means it, too. He's only got Andrey for an heir."

Arranging a marriage with the Kastavas' eldest daughter signaled a permanent union between the families. Once they married, the Kastavas would no longer be identified as our rivals but as our kin.

"I don't trust it." I opened the door Andrey had left through, holding the door open for Ivan to go first.

"Me neither," he replied, scanning the alley we'd exited to.

I assumed many more of my brothers in the bratva would be with us on this sentiment. Until someone else was in power, these disastrous ideas would continue to bring us down. I wanted to think things could change for the better, but it didn't seem likely.

Because once Andrey married his bride, there would be no way to backtrack out of whatever the Kastavas were scheming to do.

2

MILA

Today began like any other day.

I left my father's home to promptly come in to manage the front desk of the S.T.L. Shipping headquarters. Dealing with paperwork for one of the family's cover businesses was how I survived the daunting hours as they passed.

I wasn't ever idle, and that helped to keep my mind on my tasks. Business was good—both the legitimate shipping transactions and the undercover and more profitable transportation services that happened at the Colver dock. I didn't have much to do with those dealings. My father would never trust me with everything, certainly not those high-risk arrangements. All I was good for was keeping the front running. I did. My days were full of paperwork, emails, and taking calls.

This Wednesday seemed ordinary, but it would end on a sour note.

As soon as Lev, one of my father's top soldiers, entered the office and headed to the private rooms upstairs, I knew I had to be on my best behavior. I always was, anyway. I had been trained to be submissive and obedient. Acting out or being sloppy wasn't allowed. Lev was sort of like my supervisor, but he wasn't here to watch over me. He only showed up when he'd have a meeting with my father, and those came with stipulations.

Lev had escorted his wife, Rosamund. Next came Geoff, another of my father's top men. Then my father showed. Another brigadier, laughing and talking as they entered the private floor of the shipping offices.

As each of them came in and headed to the private rooms in the back up there, I kept my head down and acted oblivious. Every month, they arrived as a group. For the sake of appearances, it looked like a top-secret meeting would occur.

I knew better. Rosamund had confided in me once, explaining that the sounds they made frightened the other whores who hung around. Mistresses would get concerned. Too many men would want to be invited.

Here, with no one but me in the offices, they could have their fun as loud as they wanted. I'd once tried to use ear plugs to tune out the screams, shouts, and wails, but Geoff had noticed them when he'd left.

"Don't hide," he'd teased as he removed the ear protection on his way out after they'd all gang banged her. "I know it turns you on to hear her screaming."

It didn't. That was my *father* in there, participating. Rosamund was one year younger than me, only twenty-one, and newly married to Lev.

As the first scream cut through the air, bile rose up my throat. I rubbed my stomach, grimacing as it churned with unease. If I knew when they would decide to share Rosamund, I would simply close down the computer and head home, but they never gave any notice. They never announced when they'd show up, and tonight, I had too many emails to forward to the specific customers.

This was our life. To be a woman under the protection and possession of the Kastava Family, this was expected. Demanded. I'd grown up knowing the sanctity of marriage, and I was aware that above all else, I would be expected to obey my husband.

But this?

No. Please, no.

Hours later, just before evening fell, they exited the building. First, the brigadier and Geoff, who stormed off, cursing up a storm. Then my father exited, laughing with Lev as they came through the doors connecting to my office up front on the first floor.

"Mila."

I sat up straighter as my father addressed me. "Yes?" I sucked in my stomach and pulled in my cheeks. Anything to thwart him from commenting on my weight again. If he cut any more calories from my diet, I would faint from malnourishment.

He nodded his head to the side, indicating the door he'd just walked through. "Rosamund needs some... help cleaning up." He spoke it like it was a waste of time. Like that slender blonde should be able to handle their dicks shoved into her over and over, in any possible way. Like that young girl, barely an adult, should be stronger to withstand abuse and torture because she'd been arranged to marry an asshole.

"Yes, sir," I replied as I stood.

He lifted his hand, though, narrowing his eyes at me as he stopped me. "You keeping up with the correspondence?"

I nodded, curious about why he'd question me. I always kept up with his demands, even something as inane as forwarding emails to separate addresses with the slightest updates. Hadn't he ever heard of carbon-copying messages? Multiple emails sent at once?

A gruff grunt was all he gave me in reply, but before he left, he eyed me with a slow once-over. His lips curled in slight disgust, but he didn't comment further, leaving with Lev.

As soon as the door closed, I heaved out a deep sigh and relaxed from sucking in my stomach. I approached the front door, locking it up for the evening. In the reflection of the glass, I saw what he had seen.

Short, curvy, and scowling. I'd never been a petite girl or woman, much to his frustration, but I didn't look bad. I knew I didn't. Smoothing my hands over my dress, I took pride in my attire, how flattering my clothes were for my size.

Fuck him.

I'd lived twenty-two years with his constant belittling and judgment, but I knew he was wrong. I took care of myself. I stayed fashionable. I made sure to emphasize my tits that all the whores envied. My long locks of deep brown were sleek and glossy. My eyes were sharp, my skin smooth and hydrated.

My father was an asshole to ever try to make me feel like crap about myself, but I could take his criticism. I had to.

I headed up to the private rooms, seething about my father's attitude toward me, but the moment I entered the private rooms and saw the evidence of what Rosamund was subjected to, my lungs seized. I couldn't breathe past the utter shock and horror of what *she* had suffered at my father's hands. Her husband's hands. All of them.

"Took you long enough," Rosamund whined.

I shuttered my face, locking down on showing any emotions.

My God... I approached her, amazed that my knees didn't buckle.

Her skin was littered in red, swelling scrapes. Most bled freely, no doubt from the ropes and whips they'd used on her. Cum dried everywhere, smeared on her flesh that still bore the deep-tissue bruises from the last time they'd shared her so aggressively.

Her hands and ankles were still leashed. Cuffed tight with wires, her limbs were locked in suspension.

They hadn't even bothered to let her down.

My fingers trembled as I hurried to untwist the locks keeping her in the air. "Sorry." I hadn't delayed coming up here, truly. But if I'd known they'd left her hanging, literally, I would have run.

She snorted, gazing absently at the ceiling. One eye was puffy. The lids slitted over her eye as she waited. "No, you're not."

"That this happened to you? Yes, I am." I bet she'd once wished for a happily ever after just like I did. Daydreaming for the impossible wasn't supposed to hurt this badly.

"You mean that this *happens* to me?" She hissed, drawing in a hard breath as I freed one hand. With that wrist free, she jerked, lowering her arm to support herself with the other cuffs still on. "Because it will. Until I can fucking kill myself, this will be my life."

I swallowed hard, not in any position to scold her or even react to her harsh words. If I were in her position…

No. Not yet. I would be married off, but I couldn't count on it happening any time soon. My father wanted me slimmer so he wouldn't suffer the embarrassment of offering a fat wife to my betrothed. My father wanted me to work in the shipping office so he wouldn't have to train another who would better serve elsewhere as he tried to expand his power.

"I am sorry that this is how it is." I freed another hand, and she rested partly on the bed. The sheets were saturated with the blood that dripped from the wires bound at her wrists and ankles, but I bet the support of a solid surface had to help.

She hissed, twisting to her side the best she could.

Maybe not.

Bile rose again. The sight of her whipped and mutilated back would haunt me for days.

"That this is how it is?" She scowled at me.

"Yes. Being a wife."

"I'm not a *wife*." She cried then, angry and destroyed. "I'm a fucking whore. His whore, to pass around."

I swallowed hard, remaining hard to her plight as I freed her ankles.

"Don't try to give me any of that shit about this being my duty."

I opened and closed my mouth, stuck on what I could say to that. My *father* raped her. My *father* took her like this, like a depraved, abusive asshole. What could I say?

"I know what you're thinking. Our duty as bratva women is to please our men."

I cleared my throat as I moved to the cuff on her other ankle. "In most circumstances—"

"No. My circumstances fucking suck. And I don't want to hear you say you care."

"I do." Even if I hadn't been told to help her, I would.

"That's rich, coming from you."

I grabbed a towel to assist her to sit, then rise to her feet. With every hiss and whimper that left her lips, my heart cracked that much more. She spoke the truth. We *were* expected to serve our men. There was no escape, but this abuse she endured…

"I sincerely wish this wasn't your fate, but I can't change it."

If I could, I would. For all of us.

"The fuck you would," she bitched as she gingerly walked toward the bathroom with my assistance. "You don't care. You'll get a nice, cushy life away from your father."

He'd never tried to abuse me like he did her, but still, she was wrong. I wasn't going anywhere.

"I'll still be right here to help you the next time."

Rosamund almost fell, but I held her up. "No, you won't."

I didn't understand.

She scowled at my reflection in the mirror. "You're pure. You'll remain untouched as a virgin. You've always been safe, expected to be a virgin."

"As were you."

"Yes. Safe—until your husband gets you."

Not every man in the bratva wanted to share his wife.

"I'm sorry you were promised to Lev."

She huffed a weak laugh. "I was talking about *your* husband."

Mine? I shook my head, watching her carefully as I guided her into the shower. "I don't have one."

"You will. Soon." She cried out at the first touch of the water spray.

"I don't believe you." This wouldn't be the first time she'd tried to lash out verbally at me after the scenes forced on her. "My father would have told me."

"When? When he was busy shoving his dick up my ass?" She moaned and leaned against the shower wall.

"I'm too vital with the S.T.L. and making it look like a real business. He wouldn't get rid of me yet. I'm too critical in the office." Besides, he'd claimed I was too fat and hideous yet.

"I heard them. As they…" She weakly gestured at the room she'd been abused in. "They were talking about it. Geoff didn't want to hear about it." She grimaced as she rubbed the blood from her chest. "Lev and your father discussed your marriage to Andrey Valkov."

I froze in rolling up my sleeves to hand her the washcloth to tend to cleaning up the cum and blood.

Andrey Valkov? Heir to the Valkov Bratva? Our enemy?

With how angrily Geoff had stormed off tonight, that made sense. He'd always been eager to have me for himself. This news wouldn't have pleased him.

"Valkov?" I knew my father was speaking with Pavel Valkov, but about my marriage to his son?

Please, no.

I'd heard too many horror stories about him. He was reported to be a hard, sadistic, and greedy man. As I helped Rosamund clean off, I wondered how much worse I would fare with him. Here, my standing as the Pakhan's daughter kept me untouched. There? With the enemy? I dreaded it.

"When?"

Rosamund looked me in the eye, perhaps pitying *me* now. "Friday."

So soon! I hardened myself to the shock and drew in a deep, steady breath. My father planned to marry me off at the end of the week, and I was only learning of it now.

"It's your duty, Mila." Her tone dripped with sarcasm, cruel and mocking. "Are you going to be a good wife for him? Please and obey your husband, no matter the circumstances?"

I stared right back at this tortured woman. Neither of us could escape this life. All I could do was remain icy and numb and take it all.

Nodding once, I resolved to overcome my circumstances and beat my odds—no matter how awful they might be.

But deep inside, my heart chipped and cracked just a little more.

3

ALEK

My uneasiness about this potential alliance with the Kastavas didn't dissipate. Over the night, it worsened. By morning, when I was due to report in to my uncle for a so-called meeting with the top soldiers and brigadiers, I was anxious.

No one would know it by looking at me. The day I received word that my father died, I mastered the fine art of masking my emotions. I'd never believed the story I was given. That Pyotr Valkov, my hard-working father, had been killed in friendly fire during a turf war. None of my brothers believed it either, but with time, we had no choice but to accept it as fact. They'd questioned it. Maxim, my youngest brother, had still been more of a boy than a man when our father was killed. We all struggled in our own ways, but I knew that expressing my feelings would only be a weakness, a tell.

When I arrived at the restaurant, I was in a lousy mood. The grave and irritated expressions on the wait staff didn't improve my attitude. I caught more than one of them complaining about Pavel treating them like shit, like indentured servants, not professional waitstaff, and I could almost sympathize with them. But weren't we all in the same boat? He treated us all like peons, never hesitant to remind us that he was the boss and we would always be inferior. Dissent had been growing for a long while, and within that low morale, I had company.

It wasn't just me. My brothers often echoed my sentiments. I wasn't a lone complainer, but some days, I felt like I was the only one who'd ever think about fighting back.

"About time," Pavel said as a greeting. He wiped his napkin at the corner of his mouth then tossed it to the table. Everyone else was seated, but it seemed he and Andrey were the only two who had an appetite to touch the food.

I made a show of glancing at my watch. "I'm ten minutes early."

He shrugged as though to say *whatever*. "Seeing as we're all here now, I have two matters of business to discuss."

Such gatherings were an excuse for him to hear himself talk. He didn't know what the hell was happening with the family anymore. He didn't care.

Nikolai raised his brows at me in greeting, and I moved to stand next to him, off to the side. Ivan and Dmitri sat in front of us, and Maxim fidgeted in a seat down the opposite end of the long table. It didn't matter where we were, I always made sure to check on my brothers. I'd promised my father I would always look out for them, but I felt like I was failing at that. Letting them stay with the bratva seemed like I was permitting them to be dragged down.

"First, the fucking cartel." Pavel scowled, shaking his head slowly. "The fuck do they want?" Then he pointed at Andrey. "And the goddamn Italians. Good work, eliminating that spy at the warehouse."

Ivan leaned back, catching my eye and deadpanning. This wasn't the first time Andrey had taken credit for something he hadn't done, and it wouldn't be the last.

"They keep creeping on our territory. Interfering with our businesses. I'm sick and fucking tired of their meddling."

Big words from a little man. I maintained my blank expression while I fumed inside. If the asshole ever *tried* to keep tabs on patrols, our soldiers, any intel reports, maybe things would be different. He liked to talk big but act on nothing.

"Which is how the Kastavas will help us." He nodded sagely, losing the scowl and replacing it with a smug smile.

"They'll agree to guard our land?" a top soldier asked.

"No." Pavel sat up straighter. "They have docks on the other side of the city. Specifically, the Colver dock. We'll be able to run transportation much easier there. Our shipments won't be as susceptible to falling into the wrong hands." He pounded his fist into his hand. "The cartel and the Italians can fuck off with trying to interfere there. The law enforcement too."

The NYPD was always on our asses. The DEA too.

Still, it sounded too good to be true. I couldn't shake this skepticism, but Nikolai beat me to voicing it. "Why would Sergei Kastava want to help us at all?

"Isn't there bad blood between the families?" Dmitri asked before Pavel could respond to the first question.

Pavel scrunched his face, waving both of my brothers off. "That was from generations ago. It's not a big deal now."

Everything from the past could come back and bite us in the present. He was a delusional idiot to think otherwise.

"Besides, we have a solid agreement that's nearly finished now. Andrey and I have negotiated to barter their dock use for a portion of the arms shipment from Columbia. It's the biggest shipment we've arranged yet, and we stand to profit generously."

Maxim drummed two fingers on his thigh. As soon as I noticed the tell that Pavel and Andrey wouldn't be able to see from their side of the table opposite my brother, I narrowed my eyes. He was nervous. Or eager to speak up but too intimidated to protest. He didn't carry as much clout as the rest of us brothers did, but he was no fool. Something was bothering him about these details. I made a mental note to speak with him after this meeting concluded.

"And that brings me to the second announcement." Pavel clapped his hand to his son's shoulder. "Andrey will marry Sergei's eldest daughter. It will mark a union for life." He grinned, glancing around at us all. "They can't turn on us later if we're all family, right?"

Some of the men shared in his humor, chuckling and unworried. Ivan and I already knew, since Andrey couldn't keep his mouth shut last night. Even if this were the first I was hearing about it, I wouldn't have reacted.

"Not the most attractive girl," Pavel commented with a smirk, "but that hardly matters."

Andrey nodded, sighing. "I'd do anything for the family."

Oh, cut the shit. Stop acting like you're some kind of martyr.

Pavel patted his shoulder again, then turned to face me. "While we're busy with the final wedding preparations, I need someone to speak with their man about this shipment." He pointed to me, then Nikolai. "You two can handle that, can't you?"

Like we're not already out on the streets and actually keeping an eye on our turf already. I nodded. "We can."

"It's nothing more than making a show of faith, checking in and seeing that everything is running according to plan. Ask for someone named 'The Doc' and inquire about whether they're ready for the big shipment."

Who the hell is The Doc? He can't mean an actual doctor. Using codes seemed weird. We weren't in the habit of relying on nicknames, and it only made me more suspicious.

I tilted my head to the side, eying my uncle sternly. "Is there a chance something won't go as you expect?" I doubted he would voice an honest concern about a potential backfire or hiccup. He was too proud to ever admit a flaw.

"Of course not. Just a pleasantry. To check in. To make sure they're getting on board with our stopping by more often."

"The agreement hasn't gone through yet," Dmitri warned.

"But we are further from being rivals," Pavel insisted. "Just go for a show of fucking faith," he ordered of me and Nik.

Faith? He wanted to talk about faith? How about instilling it in us for him? If he could provide any details or reasons we should consider this at all, I bet a few more might lose their doubts.

Pavel stood, buttoning his jacket as he narrowed his gaze at me. "Can I not trust you to handle this? A simple request?"

Before I could reply, he smirked. "Your father wouldn't have questioned me."

My father wouldn't have tried to align with our oldest rival, either.

"Consider it done," Nik said for both of us. He grabbed my sleeve, roughly directing me to the side, near Maxim. "Tone it down," he warned in a heated whisper.

I ignored his knowing look and the scolding energy behind it. I didn't care if Pavel became annoyed with me. It was a habit by this point.

Men filed out of the private dining suite, but Nik and I remained near Maxim. We'd both noticed his nervous tell during those announcements, and Nik pounced on him as soon as we were off in the corner, able to have a private moment. "What's wrong?"

Maxim glanced past Nik, checking on the others still filing out. I nodded, letting him know we would be in the clear to speak freely.

"We will struggle to give the Kastavas the agreed-upon arms. I've seen the details in some emails I've caught in correspondence. Pavel's not sharing much about these negotiations, but I've seen bits here and there."

I believed him. Maxim had held a position with the bookkeepers for years now. His forte was the office work, everything that happened behind the scenes to make all our transactions—legal or not—run smoothly.

"The books look bad. I don't know all the codes of their messages. Regardless, from the books I've seen and worked on, things are grim."

"How so?" Nik asked.

"We don't have enough money to secure enough guns coming from Columbia. When the shipments arrive, the Kastavas will get the short end of the stick with this deal. We'll already be using their Colver dock, as agreed, but what they'll see at that dock will be less that what they're told they'll get."

I rubbed my jaw. Unease and doubt prickled up my spine, and I knew my hunch, that bad feeling I couldn't shake, was a real and sincere concern.

"Does Pavel know?" Nik asked.

Our uncle wasn't a fan of being told bad news, and I wondered this same thing, whether Maxim, or another bookkeeper, had already shared these facts and it was dismissed.

Maxim cringed and nodded.

"I bet the Kastavas know too." If Pavel were capable of duplicity, maybe they wouldn't, but Pavel wasn't that bright. "They likely know and intend to use it as leverage."

"What are you saying?" Maxim asked.

"I suspect they're planning a coup. This alliance smells rotten."

"But as soon as this wedding takes place… it won't matter. They'll be family whether we want them to be or not."

I was already suspicious about the shipping plans, but if it's as bad as my brother warned, this could be the fuck-up that brought the entire Valkov operation down.

"Unless the wedding *doesn't* take place…" I glanced at them both as the idea took root. "If we're not united with them yet, I could try to look into this arrangement."

"You mean to stop the wedding?" Ivan asked.

I shrugged. *It's not a bad idea.* All I needed was more time to figure out how to avoid the potential downfall of our family.

4

MILA

This would be the last day of my freedom, and I struggled to accept that I was spending it at home.

Freedom? I'd never had any true sense of that fantasy. I lived with my father ever since my mother passed away while giving birth to me. He controlled me at home and here at one of his excuses for a business.

Friends were denied to me. I was educated by private tutors. Pastimes and hobbies weren't allowed.

My existence was nothing but serving the family, and now that my allegiance would need to shift, to cater to my husband, I felt untethered and unsure of everything.

I'd never have to come here again and suffer through the tedious task of forwarding certain emails to specific addresses. It was mindless, ridiculous busywork, but it gave me a tangible sense of purpose. I was active. I was *doing* something. I didn't want to entertain what expectations would hang over my head after my wedding.

How can it be tomorrow? It was too soon for me to possibly adjust. My father told me just this morning, almost like an afterthought, before he left for meetings with Lev and Geoff.

How can my life be changed this drastically on such a short notice? I'd grown comfortable in this pathetic desk job, and now that the security and familiarity of it would be yanked away, I felt lost and apprehensive.

"The 'Doc'?" I whispered aloud, furrowing my brow at the screen. Some of these coded references made no sense at all, but I gave up trying to understand who or what " The Doc" was, why an "understanding needed to be proven," or how "unwarranted hardware ratio shifts" mattered. I didn't follow this jargon, and I didn't want to. I wasn't trusted with too many things, but my father had been adamant that I specifically handle this looping correspondence. I assumed someone else, maybe my father, was watching what was said where, as he had my passwords, but it wasn't my business. I'd learned long ago not to ask questions. Since my father singled me out to handle these emails, I assumed that he didn't want many to know, even within the family.

Whatever.

I couldn't even care anymore. I never had, but mere curiosity just didn't matter. All I could obsess about was whether my life would change for the worse tomorrow.

Two men approached outside, and their appearance snagged my attention. This was a front business, with mock shipping for general items. Visitors seldom came by, but these two tall men did not look like lost solicitors.

On the left, a muscled brute strode toward the door. He'd spotted the surveillance camera that allowed me this preview of their arrival, and his lips almost kicked up in a smile. Or was that a smirk?

His companion, a blond, didn't hide his eyes behind sunglasses. He scoped his surroundings, those blue eyes not stopping on anything long enough.

It hardly mattered why they were here. This was protected land. They were strangers letting themselves onto Kastava territory. I minimized the window on my computer and locked it as I shot to my feet.

I couldn't understand how the guards or patrolmen wouldn't have stopped them from coming to the S.T.L. Shipping office, but I supposed it was up to me to deter them from snooping around here any further.

They opened the door and entered. At once, I realized who they were. I didn't know their names. I'd never seen them in person before, but I recognized the tattoo on the taller one's neck. Sloping along the taut muscles, the ink linked lines and swirls in what had to be the Valkovs' crest.

The enemy.

"You can't come in here." I crossed my arms.

"I *can't?*" The man lifted his sunglasses to bore me with his serious, sinister stare. "Looks like we can. And we just did."

"Alek." His companion sighed, like he was used to this smartass. "Enough of that mood."

"Mood? That's what you call... that?" I gestured one hand at the hulking man. With muscles galore, he was a tall, towering giant. Power radiated from him, and I knew without a doubt that he had to be one of the Valkovs' high-ranking soldiers. "You need to leave."

Alek tipped his chin up, looking down his nose at me. I'd never been a petite woman, but I'd always been cursed as too short. I'd be damned if I craned my neck to meet this jerk's gaze. I ignored him, doing my damnedest to curb the instant urge to check him out. Instead, I faced the almost kinder one. He couldn't be a nice man, but he seemed calmer, not ready to fight me or argue semantics. "You need to leave," I repeated.

Even though I tried speaking past him, addressing his friend, Alek stepped closer and closer.

I lowered my arms as I retreated toward my desk. Instinct had me leaning back, holding the edge of the furniture for support. The nearer Alek came, the less I remembered why I shouldn't stand up tall and order him out.

His cologne teased my nose, but the scent of *him*, so raw and masculine, called to me. Heat exuded from him, warming me in this overly chilled room with fans and the AC. As he towered over me, glaring down and locking me in the spell of his intense stare, I wasn't shy about why I should kick him out.

If he took one more step closer, I'd be caged in. The thrill of that idea sparked a flare of desire. I felt it in my pussy. In my nipples. I'd been surrounded by many virile, strong, and gorgeous men in my life.

None of them had ever instigated a rapid and visceral reaction like *this* before. I kept my lips closed and refused to show a flicker of awareness. He couldn't know. I couldn't go weak now. Not with the enemy.

"*You* think you've got the right to tell *me* what to do?"

I lifted my chin, clinging to defiance as he challenged me. "In here, yes, I do."

"I don't take orders from young girls like you." He leaned his head to the side a bit, looking me over and lingering with his dark gaze on my breasts. With how deeply my chest heaved, I wanted to cringe at how hot and bothered he was making me.

Just like that. Zero to sixty. He had me craving his presence, and I didn't like feeling so unsettled with it.

No. This isn't happening.

They couldn't get to anything here. Since I'd locked the computer, they couldn't find anything of value here. Still, I knew what was expected of me. Allowing Valkovs to sneak around here would be an unforgivable mistake.

"Alek. Enough, I said."

"Fuck off, Nik. I came here to speak with The Doc, not wait for some sex kitten to tell me what I can or can't do."

Sex kitten? I knew this dress had a lower cut than my others, but I was no—

"What did you say?"

He narrowed his eyes at me. "You heard me. Sex kit—"

I shoved at his hard chest, jarred from the haze of lust he'd so quickly put over me. *The Doc?* What a coincidence. "No. Why are you here?"

"We're here to speak with someone about a shipment coming soon," Nik said as I walked around my desk.

Putting the piece of furniture between us would be a good buffer, but with the intense way Alek continued to lock his gaze on me, I didn't feel much safer.

"With The Doc," Alek reminded me.

I shook my head. "There's no 'Doc' here." I had no clue if his wording tied into what I'd just seen on the computer, but I had to remain suspicious, if oddly drawn to his dark stare and warm proximity.

"You sure you know what you're talking about?"

I narrowed my eyes. "I know what I'm talking about when I tell you to leave. This is Kastava territory, Valkov."

He nodded, rubbing his jaw. "Haven't you heard? We're about to be united."

My throat went dry. Words couldn't come. *As a matter of fact, I have heard, asshole.* I was expected to be a key player in this union, but the more I thought about how bad my life would become as Andrey Valkov's wife, the harder I wished for something else.

It didn't matter that the clock was ticking away. Deep down, I clung to the fantasy that my marriage might not go through. If these men assumed the engagement would happen, it looked like I had to give up on that farfetched hope.

I replayed Alex's taunt in my mind again, though, leaning heavier on how he'd said it. *We're about to be united.* I could vividly imagine it. Uniting as one with *this* cocky Valkov. Sliding against him and taking his dick inside me until we were joined in the most intimate, deepest way possible.

Once more, he dragged his attention over me. His stare sparked with more than annoyance at my talking back. He checked me out with a raw hunger that almost excited me.

"We've come under the orders from Pavel Valkov," Nik said, trying for a more diplomatic but still stern tone.

I nodded, but caught myself and shook my head. "That may be so, but there is no one here to meet with you."

"Your father?" Alek guessed.

I shook my head.

"Your superior?" he tried again.

"It's just me here."

He huffed, rolling his eyes. "Well," he said as he turned slightly to face Nik, "*she* can't be The Doc."

Again, that reference to something in the emails. This was the bratva, not some rough MC gang. We didn't use road names or aliases like that. Maybe the Valkovs did, but I wasn't informed of anything they might be here for.

"Regardless, you need to leave." I pointed at the door, proud that my finger didn't tremble.

"You always this bossy?" Alek retorted.

"Until any marriage takes place between our families—"

"Sounds like it's a done deal." Alek shoved his hands in his pockets.

I pressed my lips together, exhaling hard through my nose. I didn't want to believe it yet. Until I was walked down that aisle, I had to believe something else was in store for my life.

"Until anything can bring our families together, you need to leave. No Valkovs can come lurking around here. Wait outside for whoever you think you're here to meet." I pointed again, aiming my finger at the window, indicating that they could go toward the street.

I was alone here, but I was no dainty fool. I had to be firm with these men. Especially the rugged man who continued to stare at me so closely, so heatedly that his focus felt like a naughty caress over my skin.

Nik's phone rang, and he frowned down at it. When he moved the device to his ear, he nodded once, dipping his chin at me. He sighed and headed for the door, elbowing Alek on the way. "Come on."

He didn't move. Lingering right there, boring me with his dark-brown gaze, he seemed to struggle with the need to leave.

Finally, with an expression full of suspicion and doubt, he turned and followed Nik back outside.

I didn't hurry to lock the door after it closed. Instead, I stared at the small monitor on my desk that showed me they were leaving as I'd demanded.

Alek turned, though, glancing up into the cameras once more, almost as though he had to have the last look, one final act of being a rebel and not hurrying away.

I sighed then bit on my lip as I considered the chance I could see him again once I married into his family. Would that flame of desire rise again? Could my husband be just as sexy, luring me with that immediate magnetism like Alek had?

Would this instant lust die out so I could please my husband instead?

Shaking my head, I sat. Then I dropped my face into my hands. I wasn't sure what to make of their visit.

All I knew was that I wasn't ready to get married despite the minutes ticking by to bring me closer and closer to that exact fate.

5

ALEK

My brothers would be stopping over later to speak with me, but I had a few hours to kill before they'd show up. Even though we were supposed to all be on the same team, working for the same family, my brothers and I had always stuck with each other. Without any real leadership from our uncle, and even less from Andrey, it felt like we were all operating loosely within chaos.

Like those Rossinis who thought they could get away with trying to bully a couple of shop owners we protected on our turf. Mr. and Mrs. Markov were one couple among many of the mom-and-pop shops in the Valkov territory, a cover business for us to launder money faster. With that protection in place, it never should have escalated to those Italian thugs coming by and trying to steal and harass from their store. If any of us had been delegated to patrolling and checking in more often, the elderly couple could have put an end to that bullshit months ago.

I was glad Mrs. Markov had the smarts to call Nikolai earlier. Even though I disliked the unfinished way I'd been pulled from that feisty woman at the S.T.L. Shipping office, I was proud to do my duty for the families the bratva represented. Nikolas kept the husband and wife preoccupied in the back while I taught the Rossinis a lesson. One might never father children again with the bat I'd used on his crotch, and I bet his partner was pissing his pants with the pain of my dislocating both arms.

My goal had been to avoid any blood spilled. It wouldn't do to dirty up the Markovs' shop and make them clean it up. Still, I bore the signs of a gritty fight. My knuckles were scraped and raw from pummeling those two Italians with my fists, and I nursed them now, dipping them into a bucket of ice water.

Had that call not come in, though, I wondered how far I would have tried to push my luck with that woman. So short, but packing a full package of the sexiest curves, gorgeous tits, and fine ass. She was the kind of woman to pound without mercy, able to take a good, hard fuck. I envisioned it clearly in my mind. How her plump red lips would wrap around my cock, her slender throat would strain as she swallowed me down. Her long, glossy locks of the deepest brown would coil nicely in my hand as I drove into her cunt.

And that sass. That attitude. If she could stand up to me and talk back like that in the office, she promised to be even hotter and daring between the sheets.

Or not.

She looked so damn young, but she had to be of legal age to even be in that office on her own. I couldn't believe how Sergei or any of his men would let a beautiful, sexy woman like her work unattended. She had seemed knowledgeable, quick to inform us that we shouldn't have come there. Behind the flicker of attraction I noticed in her crystal-blue eyes, I spotted the alarm. Confusion, even, but she masked her emotions well. It only made me that much more suspicious. She was guarding something to be that confrontational from the get-go. Maybe she didn't know all the details, but she had me more convinced that something fishy was going on.

The man we were supposed to see, Lev, ended up changing his mind about a meeting. Pavel texted me that information after the fact, and even that bothered me. This Lev couldn't be a man of his word and see through a simple check-in and chat with us? That didn't bode well.

As I wiped my knuckles off, I knew deep down that I couldn't let this happen. This big shipment at the Colver docks. Any alliance with the Kastavas. The wedding. It all seemed off. Over the years, I'd complained about how our power and influence had faded, but this seemed like the big thing that would be our downfall.

"You home?"

I looked toward the door of my apartment at Andrey's knock and yell. This was the only one of my personal properties that my cousin knew about. Even that was telling, that I hid all of my addresses from Andrey and Pavel. The distrust ran deep in my bones.

Without answering in a verbal reply, I headed to the door and opened it a bit. "What do you want?"

"What's this bullshit I hear about you telling Anton that *you* and Ivan killed that spy at the warehouse?" He stormed in, all bluster and cocky arrogance.

Oh. The Italian I took care of, the death that he took credit for. "I didn't say a fucking thing." It wasn't my fault that another bratva brother assumed that Andrey hadn't actually done anything about that spy. They all knew how worthless he was.

"If my father asks, *I* handled it. You understand?"

I understood that he wanted to look good. But that didn't matter anymore. "Whatever. I don't give a fuck. Take credit for it."

He squinted at me, skeptical that I'd agreed so quickly.

"As long as you forget about that wedding tomorrow." I shook my head. "They're plotting against us. I can tell. You've got to convince your father that aligning with the Kastavas will be a mistake."

He scoffed. "That's the stupidest thing I've ever heard. They've been talking about it for a month."

Which was not a long enough time for true negotiations. Not that he'd know. "They're not to be trusted."

He stalked up close, trying to get in my face and look down at me. It might have been easier to pull off if I weren't slightly taller, stronger, and more ripped. "We'll decide who can be trusted." He grimaced, wrinkling his face. As he tipped his head to the side, maybe trying to look macho and bold, his bald head gleamed from the lights overhead. "That's not your call. We make the decisions. Not you."

"You'll regret it." I didn't flinch, didn't budge.

"Are you threatening me?"

"The entire family is threatened with Pavel's idea to team up with the enemy."

"Fuck you." He shoved at me, but his sneering attitude had already pushed me too far. I grabbed his hand when he pushed, then followed up with punching his face.

"The wedding's tomorrow, you dumbass." He lunged forward, entering in a quick, hard fight. My fists didn't need more damage, but I didn't hesitate to land him on his ass near the door.

"Call off the wedding," I growled as he stood. "Stop this alliance."

He shook his head, then spat a mouthful of blood onto my carpet. "Fuck off." Then he wrenched the door open and left, slamming my door shut.

I stood there, fuming and staring at the splatter of a mess he'd left on my floor. Talking reason with him wouldn't have ever gone over well. He didn't listen to anyone but his father. He couldn't comprehend anything complex even when shown evidence. Spoiled by being sheltered and expected to sit back while others did the dirty work, Andrey was unapproachable for anything against what Pavel told him.

My mind returned to the sex kitten in the office. I couldn't erase the image of her low-cut dress and bold confidence to show off her body in that sharp business attire.

Could she help? It felt like I was reaching for anything and grasping for straws, but I wondered if I could convince her to stop the Valkov-Kastava wedding. She was aware enough of the family politics to warn us away. Her intelligence was obvious, and within reason, her independence, too. Women couldn't call the shots. We lived in a world where men ruled, even idiots like Pavel here. Still, that woman had backbone.

Maybe I could ask her to tell the bride not to go through with this wedding. I wasn't above bribing her. Anything.

I shook my head and began cleaning up the smear on my floor. What was I thinking? It was ridiculous. Asking the enemy to stop this alliance would be suicide, but I was desperate to prevent more damage.

Dmitri and Nikolai showed up shortly after I cleaned the spot on the rug. They knocked with our standard code of raps, and I let them in.

Dmitri paced immediately, his heel pushing down on the now-clean spot on the floor. Nik slumped onto my couch, leaning forward to rest his face in his hands.

"Now what?"

"We're nervous about this alliance," Dmitri said.

"I went undercover and spied near their Colver dock," Nikolai said.

I gave him a hard look. He was the most skilled with disguises, but I'd warned him to be careful before. Here I was, debating what to do, and he'd just gone out and snooped.

"I watched his back," Dmitri said before I could lecture them.

That helped, but still, I had to know my brothers were as safe as possible. They couldn't be reckless. "And?"

"I got word about this tradeoff being a trick. They seemed to count on things going wrong. I wish I could have gotten ahold of the papers they were checking off and whatever they were scrolling through on their phones. I don't know." He set his hands on his knees, tense. "I'm worried it's a setup."

We'd had many issues with the cops before. They made it a habit to track our shipments and interfere, hence why having the Colver dock would be a benefit.

"Me too. If not a setup, a coup. Something. I don't trust any of this."

"Ever since Father died near the Kastava territory…" Dmitri didn't return to his thoughts. Pacing and shaking his head, he was lost in his memories of the turf war when our father was gunned down. All of us brothers suspected a setup, and this felt like déjà vu. A setup again.

"I won't let them bring us down. Pavel has abused his position of power for too long. If he is blind to this being a potential setup, or worse, then I'll do what's right."

Nik stood and glanced at Dmitri. "How?"

"First, I'm stopping that fucking wedding." It would connect us too deeply, too irrevocably.

"The shipment isn't due to come until next week," Dmitri added. "Maybe stopping the wedding would throw off this shipping arrangement from even happening."

I shrugged. It'd incite war to prevent Andrey from marrying Mila Kastava. But I'd do it. Andrey and I had always been pitted against each other. We were the top two cousins, and if I intervened with his marriage, all kinds of uproar and inner fighting would follow.

"We support you," Nikolai said unnecessarily.

"The men will too," Dmitri vowed. "Whatever you can pull off, however you can prevent the bratva from crumbling completely, you can count on us."

I nodded, more confident with his words. Morale had been low. It wouldn't take much to adjust the power in our family.

First, though, was canceling this wedding. And hopefully, that would buy me more time to figure out about this supposed alliance and risk of a setup.

6

MILA

In order to be fitted for my dress, I headed home early from the S.T.L. headquarters. It was a bittersweet experience, saying goodbye to those four walls of the shipping office. For the last three years, that place was my purpose. After tomorrow, my role in life would be different. I had yet to learn what I could expect as Andrey's wife, but my guesses didn't fill me with hope.

So long as he doesn't plan to treat me like Lev does Rosamund...

I sighed, banishing the thought as I stood on the dais.

"Can't you" —the seamstress winced— "suck it in?" She tugged at the fabric over my torso.

I knew she meant my stomach, but that wasn't the issue. My hourglass curves were tricky to tailor too, but she wasn't getting away with talking to me like that. "My tits?" I snapped. "Not sure how I can suck them in."

She sneered at me. "Just—"

"Wouldn't expect *you* to know." As soon as the catty words left my mouth, I regretted them. Snapping back at people, even a seamstress ordered to do this fitting so quickly, wasn't how I was trained to be. It wasn't my nature to be so bitter and bitchy like this. It wasn't her fault I was stuck in this position. I couldn't take my frustration out on her for what I had to do.

Tipping her chin up, she resumed fitting my dress to me. An hour later, she seemed satisfied with her speedy handiwork. My nerves scaled higher with each minute that passed, and I regretted not eating earlier. I couldn't have, anyway. My father insisted that I fast and try to look slimmer for the memorable day tomorrow. Anxiety swirled in my empty stomach, and I wished I could rub it. It had taken a dozen barked orders not to mar the dress for me to remember that I couldn't give myself any comfort.

My father was asked to enter and check the quality of the dress before I could take it off. His opinion mattered, not mine. It was his image that counted, not mine. I was a pawn, but dammit, I wanted to rip these stupid lacy sleeves off already.

He entered, not smiling or allowing any reaction to show on his face. With impatience and the usual glare of scorn and disapproval, he looked me over. "I suppose it's the best you can do."

"Given the hasty timeline—"

"Not the rush." My father barely glanced at her, giving me his full annoyance. "The best you can do with *her*."

I refused to react. Standing still with my chin held high, I ignored her slight gasp.

"Oh. Well, um…" She was caught in this tense, awkward moment, but I didn't want her pity. Maybe this marriage could be a blessing. I'd get away from his mental abuse, at least.

"Come see me in my office after you hang that up." Without waiting for a reply, he turned and left the room.

"Sorry," the seamstress said as she helped me out of the gown.

Pity. Just what I didn't want. It would do me no good, anyway. I didn't reply, acting like I hadn't heard her low murmur, and quickly dressed in my office wear again before heading to speak with my father.

Given the last-minute manner that he told me I was getting married, I dreaded to think of what other afterthoughts he'd neglected to tell me.

I closed the door to his office and waited, standing with my hands clasped in front of me. A docile, dutiful daughter. That was the persona I projected, but in my heart, I trembled for more bad news.

"Any thoughts on your marriage?" he asked.

I blinked, not quick enough to mask my surprise. He was *asking* for my opinion? Did he actually want to know? It was impossible.

"Do you have any thoughts about your marriage?" He wasn't repeating that question with a firmer, more impatient tone to hear me tell him that I didn't want it to happen. That I wished I could marry for love, not duty.

"I'm nervous." All I could do was speak the truth. "But I will see it through if that is what you wish."

He nodded, stroking his beard.

"I believe this marriage will be a mistake."

He huffed, smirking as he leaned back in his chair. "It will not be a mistake. Regardless, you are to do as expected. You will marry the heir to the Valkov Bratva. You will bear him a son."

I swallowed hard, afraid of *that*. My main concerns were how that consummation would occur. Losing my protected virginity to a rough man like Andrey scared me, but he didn't want to hear about it. I had no one to talk to. No one to seek comfort from. My mother died right after my birth, and no woman in the family had ever stepped in as a maternal figure I could rely upon.

"Do you understand me?"

"Yes." In the back of my mind, I screamed for the opposite. I resisted the urge to ask if there was any other way to secure this alliance.

"I can't hear you."

I cleared my throat and raised my voice to more than a whisper. "Yes, sir."

"After the wedding, I expect you to report back to me."

What? I furrowed my brow before I caught myself and resumed a blank expression. "Report to you?"

He nodded, irritated that I'd questioned him.

"Am I a spy or a bride?"

"You are my daughter, my eldest child, and you are mine to order however I see fit. Even if you're married."

I narrowed my eyes at him, unsure what was going on. "That's not true, though. My husband will be the boss of me."

His only reaction was a smirk. If I wasn't mistaken, he'd almost rolled his eyes too.

How can he not agree? I couldn't make sense of this odd conversation. Husbands were to be the bosses of their wives. Their rulers. As soon as Andrey and I vowed to be a couple, he'd own me. He'd control me.

Why would he think he'd be the exception? To still order me around after I left his home?

"Have I made myself clear?"

I nodded but stopped halfway. "Report to you about what?" My suspicions deepened. A firm sense of confusion clouded my mind as I tried to understand. I couldn't see how he planned to override my husband's wishes, but more than that, what information was he seeking to obtain from me?

"You will know," he responded vaguely.

I will? He never confided in me anything, and I felt like I was not only a pawn in a game I didn't know the rules for, but also a sacrifice. Marrying Andrey was already a lousy circumstance to find myself in, but now I couldn't shake the hunch that I was about to be married off to an enemy, not a potential future ally. Were the Valkovs to be trusted? Would I be a player in a twisted, covert mission, sneaking into their family?

I didn't want to marry an enemy or an ally. If I could choose, I'd opt to marry someone out of love, out of fondness. Hell, I'd settle for a pairing based on desire. What I'd heard of Andrey and what I'd seen in pictures didn't suggest lust or love. His reputation as a hard, brutal man preceded him. Even Rosamund felt sorry for my fate.

But I bet she'd think differently if the Valkov men were all like Alek. I tuned out my father's repeated lecture about being obedient, no matter what. He'd told me the same thing over the years, and it was far better to retreat in my mind while I pretended to listen.

He droned on and on, but all I could think about was him. Alek. Still to this minute, as I was being prepared to marry another man, I felt the lingering flicker of attraction he'd ignited in me. How he'd argued with me, daring me to fight back. The way he'd looked me over with that ravenous, deep bronze gaze of his. In the span of seconds, that massive man had overwhelmed my senses and fired my libido like never before.

"Do you understand?" my father barked once more, jarring me from my thoughts about the Valkov who'd challenged me at the S.T.L. office.

I nodded, even though I had no clue what he'd said.

"Go." He flicked his hand at me, and I didn't wait for a more elaborate dismissal.

Since it was the evening before my wedding, I knew he'd excused me to my room. Going anywhere else was out of the question—and it wasn't like I had the freedom to go anywhere as I pleased. Just here at the house or the offices. And tomorrow, Andrey's home.

He was there, striding down the hallway. Almost as though my thoughts had summoned him, he appeared, his lewd gaze on me.

"Come in, come in," my father said behind me, welcoming Pavel and Andrey Valkov into his office.

My father seldom carried business at home, but seeing as Pavel would be my in-law, maybe that changed things.

"In a minute." Andrey continued on, passing my father's office as Pavel entered and closed the door.

I dipped my chin in a hasty nod of acknowledgement, intimidated with the possessive look in his eyes.

You don't own me. Yet.

"Running off?" he taunted, hurrying to chase me down the hall.

I kept my pace even. I'd be damned if I showed him fear, but I wished I'd already reached my room before he'd shown up for their chat.

"You can't." He caught up to me, grabbing my arm and shoving me toward a shadowed turn of the hallway. "Tomorrow, you'll be mine to fuck as I please."

Both my hands were captured in one of his, and with his free hand, he groped at me, ripping my blouse to squeeze my breast hard, then sliding his hand lower to yank up my skirt.

He'd reached me so suddenly, it all flew by as a blur. As he dipped his hand between my legs, ripping my panties, he raked his greedy gaze over me.

It chilled me. His attention felt nothing like the sensual, naughty caress of Alek's eyes on me earlier.

"But there's nothing wrong with sampling your cunt tonight."

"No." I flinched at his words, knowing that he intended to rape me right here in the hall. Hatred swept over my mind, casting a dark and violent energy through me as I fought back the best I could. He was too tall, too strong, and trapped to the wall, I was unable to run.

He unzipped his pants, grunting as he tried to pull his dick out.

"Miss Kastava."

Andrey went still at the sound of one of my father's soldiers. He was a kindly older man, one my mother allegedly helped when he was shot in the house.

"Is there a problem here?" he asked.

Andrey swore, backing up as he tucked himself back into his pants. My skirt fell back down as he retreated, and I caught my breath as I realized I'd been spared.

For now.

"No. No problem," Andrey answered for me as he smiled at the soldier. "Just saying good night to my bride."

Good night, my ass.

I turned, too startled to say thank you to the guard. Running was all I could think about, but I couldn't. That display proved that my future would be as bleak and awful as I'd feared. As I paced in my room, high-strung with all this pent-up energy and adrenaline, I wished again that there were another option. Another bride to offer to them. Another man they could arrange for me.

Like Alek. The hit of desire he'd encouraged in me was so fleeting, so instant, and I wanted another dose of it.

Please, anything to avoid marrying that asshole...

My prayers wouldn't be answered. I knew they wouldn't be. Back and forth, I trekked in my room, but I couldn't relax. I couldn't sleep.

With nowhere else to go, I snuck out to do more work at the S.T.L. offices. I'd never come back here again. Whatever chores and email maintenance I did here wouldn't matter tomorrow on my wedding day. But it was all I had to distract myself, all I could do to try to stop thinking about my fate.

Codes and weird email chains. I sighed as I clicked through the route of sending the information along to the correct spots. None of it made sense. I couldn't decipher any of it, and I hardly cared, anyway.

As the night passed into morning, I kept at it regardless, vainly fantasizing about how I could solve the riddle of my life.

How I could hope for the improbable and figure out how to avoid my wedding.

7

ALEK

The day of the wedding dawned dark and stormy. It put me in a sinister mood, ready to impart some violence to ensure this union wouldn't happen. Summers were hot and brutal with the heat of the city, but as I walked the last block toward the old church where Andrey would take Mila as his bride, a cool breeze threaded through the streets.

I'd never taken stock of my surroundings with too much sentiment. I wasn't superstitious, and I didn't have the creativity to assume my environment could add to my plans. Under the cover of dark, heavy clouds and the threat of rain, though, I could easily convince myself that the setting was appropriate.

Chaos. That was what the sky promised. And that was all I intended to bring to this ceremony.

Cars lined up along the street. On the sidewalks, guests hurried inside before the clouds opened and dumped a deluge. Humidity stuck to the surface of the windows as air-conditioning units cranked at top throttle to chill the building. Even though everyone rushed inside and claimed seats, I lingered outside, stalling and waiting for my opportune moment to strike.

Last night, Nikolai and Dmitri stayed over to discuss how I could pull the brakes on this wedding. Killing the groom or bride seemed excessive, and it would be a weightier grievance than merely preventing their wedding from proceeding as planned. If I could secure evidence that the Kastavas were trying to fuck us over, Pavel wouldn't want Andrey to marry Mila. All I needed was time to prove that my suspicions were warranted. After I accomplished that, I didn't give a shit who married whom.

As long as it's not me at the altar. I snorted a laugh as I leaned up against the rough brick wall to the church. Marriage wouldn't be in the cards for me. I doubted I'd ever want to marry, and since I was only a cousin, the son of a dead man, my marriage wouldn't carry much clout for the Family. My life was better spent killing, spying, and supervising the family's businesses. I hadn't bothered to seek any women lately, but the alternative, to only have one woman to look forward to, didn't appeal to me.

Andrey disagreed. He'd already announced his intention to cheat on this Mila woman. Affairs weren't anything out of the norm, but I'd never shared that opinion. My mother was loyal to my father, and before his death, he had yet to move on from her and seek a lover after her passing when I was five years old.

Maxim was young enough to be optimistic that he could have what our parents had once shared. Our baby brother was the hopeless romantic, but I was content to stay jaded like this, alone and untethered to live my life as I saw fit.

If I were to be stuck with a woman... I shook my head and lit a cigarette as I stalled, amused that my thoughts meandered to such a silly topic. *I'd want a curvy spitfire like that secretary.*

It'd been two days now, and *still*, I couldn't get her out of my mind. I kept thinking back to her bold gaze, unflinching as she stared me down in that office. Her kissable, fuckable lips as she'd pouted and expressed her uneasiness with what I said. And the way she'd crossed her arms? That sex kitten knew what she was doing, enticing me to check out her generous tits.

Fuck. She was seared into my mind. It wasn't only her beauty. More than anything, it was her spirit, her attitude. Bratva women weren't supposed to speak up, to act out, or to argue. Yet, she had, and that fight turned me on.

I diligently remained in the shadows to watch the guests enter the church. Guards—both Valkov and Kastava men—patrolled the block. Many of them glanced at me, curious and suspicious about why I lingered there. I wasn't a mere soldier. I wasn't part of the security force.

Instead, like I'd planned with my brothers who were already inside as guests, I would disturb the peace. The moment everyone was inside, ensuring the collective threat of so many prominent bratva acquaintances sitting vulnerable under one roof, I'd head inside and unleash gunfire. I didn't intend to kill anyone. I would if I had to. The simple suggestion of violence would be enough to cause a commotion. No one would know if they were targeted. Everyone would assume they were the one being shot at. And it would work. It was the simplest pause on the wedding that would stir enough doubt from both parties. Pavel might be too stupid and insist that they resume the ceremony after they proved the gunfire was a false alarm. But I had a hunch it might spook Kastava into reconsidering until further negotiations.

And if that didn't work? I had another idea that would cause war.

"We'll have plenty to celebrate."

I turned my head, stubbing my cigarette out on the sidewalk as a Kastava soldier spoke up on the steps. Hidden by the wall to the steps up to the entrance, I was in a prime position to listen in.

"Yes, we fucking will," his companion joked back. "Sergei is wise to set this up."

Set this up? Those words raised a red flag.

"I can't believe we've scored this big," the first soldier said. "I mean, that we *will* score this big."

"Yeah. Not just a portion of the arms, but the whole shipment."

They chuckled, laughing softly among themselves. Down on the street, in the darkness, I fumed.

I fucking knew it!

They didn't plan to get a cut of the arms—arms it sounded like we couldn't afford to receive in the first place. They planned to somehow take it all.

When another man approached them, they changed the topic, discussing the security for when the husband and wife left after the ceremony was over. I tuned them out, knowing it wouldn't get to that point. I wouldn't let them. Hearing these men convinced me that I was right to suspect the Kastavas would screw us over, and I wouldn't stand by and let us get connected to enemies intending to steal from us. Or set us up. Either would end us, and it was up to me to stop it.

Enough of this bullshit. I wouldn't second-guess myself again. The Kastavas didn't want an alliance. They intended to take over.

Over my dead body. I glared at the street, biding my time until the guests were all inside. A glance at my watch confirmed that the moment neared. Any second now, the music would waft out through the slim window over my head. It would be my cue to act, and I would, ruthlessly and swiftly.

My phone buzzed. It was the text Ivan had agreed to send, a final confirmation that the key players were in place.

Ivan: ..

Two periods. It was his code for an all-clear, and I knew that to mean Pavel and Sergei were both inside, seated in the front-row pews.

I drew in a deep breath, relishing the cooler, open air out here before I left my hiding spot. Confidence filled me, not nerves. Power strummed through my muscles as I jogged up the steps. Not fear. I wouldn't hesitate, not for a second. When I made my mind up, nothing and no one would steer me from seeing my mission through.

Recognized as a top brother in the bratva, I was given clearance at the large, wooden double doors that had been pulled shut. My brothers wouldn't think anything of my presence here. The Kastavas would know better than to wonder why I came inside now. I was expected, and with that easy entrance, I headed inside the vestibule.

Incense assaulted my nose, and I winced at the old, musty stink of the ancient building. Dim light shone from the mosaic-decorated ceiling, but I didn't wait to reach for my gun. I strode over the polished marble floor, knowing many more shoes would be stampeding over the surface as they fled the burst of gunfire I'd send to the ceiling.

Ivan glanced at me. It was all the acknowledgment he'd give me. Dmitri nodded, standing at his position near another door that led into the cavernous space of the church. Near the furthest of the three doors leading into the congregations' pews was Nikolai. He rocked back on his heels, a tell for his anxiousness to move and act on a plan.

Easy. Just wait.

I walked up closer, keeping my gun tucked to my side as I scanned the church. Guests and family members waited for the wedding to begin. I saw no sign of Andrey at the altar yet, but he had to be inside somewhere.

I glanced to the left, narrowing my eyes in the direction of the rooms where I bet he would be waiting to walk out. The hallway showed no activity, no guests or Valkovs preparing to walk down the aisle.

What's taking so long? Music continued to flow from the organ. Melodic chords carried through the chilled building, and as the tempo increased, so did my heart.

Any second now.

I turned, glancing to the right to see if the bridal procession was coming from that side of the building. More rooms were positioned there, and I knew plenty of people would be attending to the stars of the day. Bridesmaids, flower girls, the bride. They had to be down there, about to enter the aisle space.

All I saw was one angry guard. He approached so swiftly, I didn't have a chance to step back.

"What the fuck do you think you're doing?"

Shit. He had to have seen my gun. I'd pulled it out too early. Or maybe not.

Fuck it. I lifted my arm, ready to pull the trigger and start the chaos. Pandemonium would follow the noise, but he stopped me.

Grunting hard, he chopped his hand down on my arm, and I spun to deflect his next hit. Just like that, we fell into an intense fight. Others rushed closer. My brothers jumped into the action, backing me up. It was madness.

Just as I pistol whipped the guard who'd first noticed me, I jerked my head up at the change of music.

The bridal march.

The wedding was starting.

The distraction cost me, and before I could refocus on firing my gun, another soldier tackled me. My gun went flying, skidding across the floor, out of reach for my first plan.

It's not over yet. I gritted my teeth, punching and kicking the Kastava assholes while I strained to reclaim my gun.

I would not let us get hitched to the enemy. Until my dying breath, just like my father had, I would fight for the bratva.

8

MILA

No matter how many times I told myself that I could do this, I wished I didn't have to.

I stared at my reflection in the room just past the vestibule of the church, and I tried to will myself to be strong. Gazing directly into my eyes, I fought to keep my lower lip from trembling.

The bridal attendants came and went. They weren't my friends. Some were cousins. Others were just bratva wives and daughters of other men within our organization. Not one of them tried to talk to me, and why would they? I was just a pawn, as were they as they fulfilled their duties in walking down the aisle. This wasn't a ceremony of love but a production, a chance for my father to show off his wealth and attention to detail.

I didn't give a shit about a single flower or strip of ribbon. The décor blurred into the rest of the details of this ornate church, and it was easier that way, to keep it all as a smear of time passing. A passage of my life as a virgin to a used-up wife.

Zoned out into my mind, I tried to lock down on a numb sense of nothingness. But I went too far, disengaging from reality as I stared into the mirror.

"Ready?" Andrey sneered as he stalked closer.

We were alone. My bridal party had left me here, probably asked to leave me with my groom when he knocked on the door. They wouldn't tell him no. No one could.

I shook my head but caught myself. "It's bad luck to see the bride before the wedding."

He hurried closer, snarling. "I don't care about fucking *luck*."

I swallowed hard, panicking as he rushed toward me. I knew he'd fill me. He'd take me hard like a cruel punishment. I saw it in his eyes. But I hadn't thought he'd take me now. I'd been telling myself to stay strong for the inevitable rape later tonight.

"No."

"Oh, is that how it's going to be?" He yanked me close as he unzipped his pants. It was déjà vu, a repeat of what he'd tried to do last night. "You think you can tell me *no*, whore?"

"Please."

"Begging." He scoffed. "That's more like it." As he pulled me closer, almost making me trip over my dress, he turned me and shoved up the many layers of my dress. "You'll beg for me to fuck you. And you'll—"

Knocks pounded on the door, and whoever stood on the other side didn't wait. My heart beat faster with the promise of rescue, but I knew that couldn't be true. It was nothing more than a delay. A pause. Because I was marrying this asshole. He would get his hands on me before the end of the night.

I sniffled, almost losing the fight with the tears stinging my eyes.

Andrey stood up, growling at the interruption. He released my dress with a hard shove, and I heard seams tear with his brutal handling.

"You're expected at the altar."

Geoff. My insides shriveled at his voice. Of all the people who could've come here seeking Andrey, of all the soldiers or guards who might have noticed Andrey letting himself into my room, it had to be him.

"Yeah." Andrey stepped back, striding out of the room. Once his footsteps sounded away, the click of the door shutting followed.

I breathed in deeper, straining to get back to that neutral blank mask I had to rely on. I wouldn't be able to get through this if I didn't force my mind and heart to remain numb.

These few moments alone would be my last. Because as soon as I left this room—

A footstep sounded on the floor.

Fuck.

Then another.

Geoff. He hadn't left the room when Andrey had.

I spun around, facing him with a stern glower. It was the catalyst he needed to rush at me, his face contorted with that same twisted scowl of lust and impatience Andrey wore.

"No. Geoff, no!"

He caught me, slamming me against the wall harder than Andrey just had.

"Don't. Geoff, no!"

"Fucking Valkov." The sharp hiss of his zipper being undone cut through the air, and I wrestled against him to get free. "He's got no right."

Through the panic, fury rose. Geoff wasn't talking about Andrey trying to rape me before the wedding. He was only mad that I was being taken from him. From home. Ever since I reached puberty, he'd tried to get in my pants, and with a last-ditch effort, he acted on his obsession now.

"A man within the ranks of the Kastava should claim your pussy. Not a motherfucking Valkov."

He was faster, maybe more frantic as he shoved my dress up. More tears rent the air, and I sucked in a sob, replacing it with a growl. "*No,* Geoff!" Twisting and wriggling, I struggled to break away. As soon as cooler air touched the backs of my thighs, I knew it would be over.

"Stop this!" A woman had rushed into the room, and between my fight to slip out of Geoff's hold and this newcomer pulling him back, she saved me.

Rosamund was there, scowling at Geoff and pushing him further back. "You stop this!"

"Fucking whore!" He slapped her, righting his clothes as he glared at her, then me. "You'll pay for that. I'll fucking make you pay for that."

She ignored him, helping me get my dress right. "I bet you will. Get out! Just go! You want the Valkovs to call war on us for this?" She gestured at me. "Taking her virginity *at* the wedding? You're insane. Get out!"

Fierce with her words, she got him moving. He cursed and muttered dark promises as he stormed out. Once the door shut, I exhaled the breath I'd been holding after my shouts.

I righted myself, smoothing my gown back down and checking in the mirror that I didn't look as disheveled as I felt. When I felt sure that I appeared the same as I had before those two men barged in, I exhaled a longer, shakier breath and glanced at her.

The makeup hid her bruises well. She looked… normal. Pissed off and ordinary. Gazing at me with an unreadable smirk, she shook her head.

"What?"

"You're…" She huffed a laugh. "Never mind."

"I'm doomed? I'm fucked? Tell me something I don't know."

She curled her lip at me, helping me with my train to get me out of the room. "You're welcome."

"Thanks," I shot back just as bitterly.

"And good luck," she sassed. "You'll need every bit of it you can get later with Andrey."

And would you believe it? My husband doesn't think luck is real.

Mine was running out. So was my time. Sweat beaded on the small of my back with every step I took down the aisle. It wasn't the bridal march playing overhead, but an ominous tune of foreboding as I approached the altar. Over and over, I flirted with the daydream of just running, picking up my dress and sprinting for the exit. I could see it in my mind. Just bolting and giving up on my duty.

One glance at my father, and I scratched that idea from my mind. He narrowed his eyes at me, disdainful as ever, but he seemed to know what I was thinking as he escorted me down the long, carpeted path.

I stemmed the tears burning in my eyes and tried my best to hold my head high. It wasn't easy. The closer I got to Andrey smiling up there next to the short priest, the more I felt like I was walking to my death. I approached a life sentence, and I wouldn't matter ever again. I never had mattered in this world where men ruled, but once I signed my life to that man, I would be a pussy to use. To dismiss.

I reached him at last, and I strained not to show the tremor in my hands as I took my groom's. His flesh was cold to touch, and the simple contact sent a chill running up my spine.

"We are gathered—"

Gunfire erupted. I gasped, stunned as I instinctively ducked down. The entire congregation reacted. Screams. Shouts. A rising din of too many people asking questions at once.

I crouched on the plush carpet over the steps of the altar, but I nearly fell face first to the surface as Andrey maneuvered me to block him. His icy grip closed on my upper arms. Digging his fingers in, he hauled me to cover his front.

He was…

He was blocking himself with my body! If I weren't so dizzy from not eating, overwhelmed with stress, and so bewildered at the sounds of violence, I would have twisted out of his reach. I wasn't a goddamn sacrifice. Not like this. Fury slid through my mind, chasing away the panic and astonishment at this coward of a man I was to marry.

My hair fell over my face, shrouding my vision. A strong huff of an exhale puffed the curls away, and as I wrenched my head up and tossed the hair aside, I witnessed the commotion.

People scrambled to duck or run. Guests and family ran toward the edges of the huge church, but coming up along the sides of the pews were two Valkovs. I recognized one as the man who'd come into the S.T.L. offices just yesterday. Niko? Something like that. My brain was too scrambled, high on stress and ruled with the instinct to fight or flee.

Up the center aisle that my father had just led me down was another man. Gun in hand, pointed at the ceiling, he fought off Kastava soldiers. He wasn't alone. Flanked by other Valkov guards and men, they hurried down the aisle.

"Stop!"

So many men shouted that order, but pandemonium had filled the entire room. My father screamed demands at Pavel. Pavel and the spineless man behind me shouted at the tall brown-haired man rushing toward us.

"What the fuck are you thinking?" Pavel's question wasn't answered.

Andrey yelled, "Alek! Stop this right now!"

Alek.

My voice faded in the back of my throat and my heart raced faster.

Alek. Aleksei Valkov.

It *was* him. My eyes weren't playing tricks on me. It was the same tall, sexy brute of a man who'd challenged me at the office. The stranger who'd elicited such a primal awareness through my body. He was here, crashing the wedding I hadn't wanted.

He locked eyes with me, and I swore I saw a moment of surprise with his recognition. He didn't seem to anticipate seeing me here, but he didn't stop. Snarling as he fought back two of my father's men, he strained and faced me again. "Get away from him!"

He was telling me to abandon my groom? At the altar, at our wedding?

I opened and closed my mouth, so shocked that I couldn't comprehend where he'd come from. Much less what he was doing. He wasn't aiming the gun at anyone, but he'd fired it and started all this chaos.

"Andrey, let her go!"

The man clutching me close like a shield didn't consider Alek's order. If anything, he pulled me snugger to his chest as it heaved with hard breaths. "Fuck you," my groom shouted back. Spittle flew from his mouth and landed on my face as he cowered behind me.

"Let her go!" Alek ran toward me, breaking free from the fighting men, and the gunfire rang out louder and faster. Valkovs fired at Kastavas, and vice versa. The fathers were surrounded, blocked by their soldiers, and Alek ran through the thick of the bloodbath.

"Go!" He ordered that single instruction to me. It was all I'd dreamed of doing. Escaping this fate. But not like this. Not in my wildest dreams did I think this enemy would come to… rescue me. I didn't even know if that was his intention. All I could tell was that he didn't want me near Andrey.

He gripped me so tightly, I couldn't wrestle away.

As Alek rushed forward and yanked me out of my fiancé's hands, the gunfire followed. They were shooting at me, not caring for a second to spare me or protect my life.

Andrey ran, giving up and seeking shelter near Pavel, but as I looked up at Alek's hard face, a searing slice cut through me. My arm flared in pain, and Alek swore, glaring down at the blood spilling over my pure-white dress. Crimson splattered and ran from the deep graze in my bicep, and I clapped my hand over the wound, breathing shallowly through my utter panic.

I wasn't used to violence *this* close. Not when it touched on my body.

"Fuck!" Alex wrapped his arm around me, ducking his head as more gunshots followed us. Not once did he let me falter, and I tried my best to run with him as he pulled me along.

Just before we reached the end of the altar, he twisted back to fire at those closest to us. Shouts merged with shots. Screams mixed into a thunderous roar of my pulse in my ears. With all the utter chaos, I couldn't think, couldn't react fast enough. All I managed was to keep running, one foot in front of the other until my knees buckled. My lungs seized, and with a sinking sense of drowning under a black inkiness, I gave up and let the sleepiness claim me, all the way down until I fell into Alek's hard arms.

9

ALEK

Maxim helped me at the side door. He lowered, hunching his shoulders as the gunfire trailed me. Bullets hit the wall. The rapid battery sent chips of the plaster raining down.

"Go. Come on." As he held the door open for me to carry Mila through, he shot back. His aim was lousy, but I appreciated his assistance. It worked, anyway. The element of surprise had helped my plans.

No one else was quick enough to chase me through here, and I bet they'd be more worried about remaining and fighting in the church. Kastava would see this as an offense, and Pavel would be busy trying to save face for one of his men.

Despite my decision to intervene, I could always count on my four brothers to have my back. I was burning all my bridges with Pavel and Andrey by foiling this wedding, but I could depend on my siblings. Others in the bratva, too. I'd only confided in my brothers about my goal to stop this wedding, but had I told the other men who reported to me, I would've had more of a following.

After Maxim slammed the door closed and shoved the lock bar on this rear exit, he caught up with me at another door that would lead through the basement and out to another hallway toward the base of the building's clock. The church was so massive that it took up a huge area of a block. And that worked in my favor. I had a car waiting on a side alley, far from where the guards would be quick to look. Maxim and Nikolai had scoped out the place for the easiest getaway.

I turned and pushed the last door open with my shoulder, careful not to jostle or drop the bride in my arms. Dust flew up with the abrupt opening of the metal panel, but I didn't slow down or care that the door flung back and banged into the brick wall. Immediately, the stench of sewage and rotten garbage wafted to me. I drew in ragged breaths, high on adrenaline and needing to hurry more.

"I'll watch the doors," Maxim said as he scanned the dark alley, shadowed by the towering church and other skyscrapers blocking out the sun. Rain pelted down faster now, almost on cue, to make this escape trickier. The drizzle from before was gone. Now, the skies poured.

I nodded my thanks. "But you need to go too. Hide." I'd given them all clear instructions. They were to take cover and wait out the aftermath. Pavel would be on a warpath, planning to get answers from them because of how close they were to me. Maxim was the least experienced with covert missions and being in the action, but Ivan and Dmitri would watch out for him.

We didn't waste any more time talking or arguing. Any minute now, Kastava's men would file out of the church. I planned to be long gone by then.

Maxim opened the passenger door so I could stow Mila in there, and I worried at how limp she was. Not dead, but out of it. Furrowing my brow, I worried for a second about how bad off she could be. I'd tried to prevent her head from knocking against the podium adjacent to the altar, but Andrey hadn't made it easy for me to reach her.

My pathetic cousin hadn't been trying to keep her for himself, but as cover.

I'd have to wait until later to think back on how it all fell apart. Dwelling on any emotions right now would be suicide. As I rounded the car and got in, I sped off with one clear objective—escape. I raced down the alley, then onto the main street.

I headed toward an apartment on the other side of the city, almost near New Jersey. It wasn't the place I usually lived, the one where my brothers—and Andrey—visited last night. This one-room studio was a private location lacking creature comforts. All of us brothers had properties we owned outside the Valkov territory, and no one else in the bratva had ever learned about them. We'd inherited them from our parents, no doubt safe hideouts my father had secured just in case.

Just in case I needed somewhere to take a kidnapped bride. My cousin's bride, the daughter of an enemy.

Her.

I glanced at her again, stunned and again suspended in disbelief that the sassy woman I saw at that dock office was Andrey's fiancée. Of all women, of all the coincidences and odd overlaps of fate, it was her.

Long, brown curls partly covered her face, but as she stirred, breathing faster, the glossy locks slid back and revealed her features. Those sharp blue eyes were hidden behind her lids, but that pouty curl of her lips, even in sleep, taunted me. Up close again, I saw her flawlessly smooth skin, the satiny swells of her cheeks, her slender neck, and down further, the generous cleavage her dress allowed.

A horn honked, and I jerked, overcompensating in a swerve as I returned my attention to the road. With the reckless maneuvering, Mila slid to the passenger door. This time, I kept my eyes on the road as I relied on my peripheral vision to reach out and barricade her with my arm. I didn't need her slumping forward, not with her wounded arm.

I had no business checking her out as I drove. In a slight panic, I checked all my mirrors, ensuring that no one was tailing me, that no one else had noticed my stupid driving.

I only had to look twice, though, and glance at her again. My eyes couldn't lie. It *was* her, and I gritted my teeth at how much more complicated this seemed to be.

Already, she was getting under my skin. I was too fucking aware of her, too intrigued and tempted. But I'd be damned if she used it against me. She seemed like just the kind of woman who'd know how to seduce a man with her gorgeous body, but I wasn't weak like that. I couldn't be. Now that I'd hit a pause on that wedding and stalled any alliance, I had to follow up and get the proof of why and how that shipment was nothing but a setup designed to bring the Valkov Bratva down.

I'd never intended to hurt the couple. Killing my cousin wouldn't have solved anything. Nor would putting a hit on this beauty. When the Kastava guards stalled me in the outer vestibule, preventing me from firing my gun and stirring chaos, I lost significant time. Once I broke away from them and burst into the actual church, my heart had nearly stopped at the sight of the pair at the altar. I'd worried I was too late, that the ceremony was already in progress. And that was when I'd reverted to Plan B.

Andrey couldn't marry her if she wasn't there.

But now that she's here with me...

I parked at the building and checked once more to see if anyone was following. No one lurked, and I hurried to get her out of the car. Even if it seemed like no one was watching, cameras could be hidden anywhere, and getting a bleeding, unconscious bride out of my vehicle would look suspicious.

Without any interruptions, I got her up to my floor. Holding her limp weight tighter against me, I unlocked the door and carried her through to the crummy, bare apartment. Minimal furniture was on offer, but this wasn't a goddamn vacation. I only needed to keep her here long enough while my brothers and I figured out the levels of duplicity behind that shipment bullshit.

After I set her on the only bed pressed up against the wall, I studied her injuries. She still hadn't woken, but I wasn't too concerned. Her stomach gurgled and growled, and with the tightness of her skin and the darker circles under her eyes, I assumed she'd simply fainted with all the commotion. Food and water would help, but all I could do was examine her head where she'd knocked it. I was no medical professional, but I wasn't too worried that she wasn't awake yet. Her chest rose and fell steadily with strong, deep breaths. I did my best not to linger and stare at the huge swells of her tits straining against the low cut of her gown. Her bloody gown.

Next, I tended to the graze on her arm. It looked worse than it actually was. Stitches would be overkill, even if I could do them myself. Although it bled quickly and a lot, I doubted her unconscious status was due to significant blood loss.

I dampened a cloth and cleaned up her arm. A long length of gauze from a first-aid kit in the bathroom helped to compress the wound, and that was the best I could do. Her gown was pink and red, ripped in a few places. But it would be fine for now. This apartment wasn't stocked with much more than the bare essentials, but I didn't plan to stay here long. I had a spare change of clothes, but they'd dwarf her.

I stood back from her and heaved out a long exhale. Finally, I could breathe. And think.

Reactions and recrimination would come swiftly. As we'd fled the church, I heard and witnessed the beginning of it. Pavel was threatening me, Sergei shouting just as furious demands. The uproar had filled the church immediately, and everything that would follow as a reaction would happen just as quickly.

Only now, behind locked doors and secure with Andrey's bride, did I let myself think back on it all as I walked back and forth. My actions would set a ripple through our world, but I'd known that going into it. I wasn't remorseful. Not an ounce of guilt hung over me that I'd intervened in a wedding.

Mila moaned lightly, stirring on the bed, and I paused in my pacing to look back at her. Maybe a small thread of worry remained for her. I hadn't intended for her to get hurt, yet what she'd suffered seemed minor.

As I thought back further to what she'd said in the office, I wondered if she would wake up mad that I'd crashed her wedding or if she'd be grateful. With the way she'd spoken in the office, I had a hunch that she was apprehensive about the union between our families. Now knowing that *she* was the bride, though, that put a different spin on it.

A headstrong and feisty woman like her didn't deserve to be used as a fucking shield for a cowardly man like Andrey.

I huffed, resuming my pacing while she slept. Now wasn't the time to be idle. I was already deep into strategizing mode, trying to guess at how this could play out. How Pavel would be reacting. I'd ousted myself from my uncle's favor, but that had been a long time coming, anyway. It felt damned good to be opposing that old fucker for once. I'd dreamed of overthrowing that bastard many times, and only the worry of what my father would have thought kept me from acting on it.

Today had been the last straw, and I'd stand by my choices.

My phone rang, and seeing that it was Ivan, I answered immediately. My brothers had been instructed to contact me when it was deemed safer, when they were away from the church.

"Ivan." I put the phone on speaker so I could hold it lower and still listen out for Mila waking.

"You've caused war," my brother greeted dryly.

I nodded, almost letting a smile cover my lips. "Good."

A longer moan and shuffle on the bed drew my attention to the woman waking up in my bed. Mila winced, blinking her expressive eyes a few times as she rolled over to see me. I watched as she surveyed the room, her gaze clouded with both shock and confusion. When her angry stare landed on me, I couldn't look away.

"Good?" Ivan replied.

"Yes. Good. War will shake things up." I let Mila look me over, and I wondered if she remembered me from earlier, either at her wedding or yesterday. If she had any memory issues from that knock on her head, it could change what I'd tell her. "I welcome war," I told Ivan. "That's what we need before anyone can ruin our Family."

Her lips twisted. Recognition dawned in her sharp eyes, and she scowled a fierce expression of red-hot anger.

The sassy spitfire was awake. I stalked over to her, curious whether she'd give me trouble.

I look forward to it. That same flame of challenge and excitement coursed through my veins, heating my blood with the allure of arguing with her again. Of seeing her riled up again.

"Call me with more news when you get it," I told Ivan before I hung up.

Right now, I had other matters to tend to.

One furious bride who glowered at me and gritted her teeth, taunting me to tell her *exactly* how this would go.

10

MILA

I woke to a throbbing ache in my head. As I gingerly brought my fingers to probe at the tender spot on my brow, I felt the mussed tangles of my hair. Then the ache of an injury in my arm.

What—

Memories streamed back to me, reminding me of the hell that had happened at the church. The tight pressure on my skin came from the tightly wound gauze that pressed against my split-open flesh.

I had been shot. I was kidnapped. My wedding…

A man spoke on the phone, and I twisted on the bed to watch his tall, powerful body pace across the simple room.

I was still so weak—dehydrated, famished, and sleep-deprived on top of the stress—but I was instantly alert at the realization that *he* wasn't a figment of my imagination.

Aleksei Valkov. The hotheaded man my libido had awakened to at the S.T.L. offices. Then the devil who'd barreled his way into my wedding, guns blazing, to steal me away.

I ground my teeth together, letting the ache of my jaw's tension add to the dull throb in my head. Through slitted eyes, I tracked his steady strides.

That asshole! Just coming in and... taking me like that!

"I welcome war. That's what we need before anyone can ruin our family."

His words sent shock and outrage slithering down my spine. *War?* He could do whatever he damn well pleased, but I didn't want to be caught in the middle of it.

Fury enveloped me. My muscles trembled with the strain of fisting my hands. The urge to launch at him and attack filled me as he disconnected his call and stalked toward me. He was predatory, striding toward me with so much masculine dominance, such sure confidence that he had me right where he wanted me.

Which is not *at my wedding.*

I didn't flinch, keeping my lips pressed together tightly as he advanced toward me. I wouldn't show him fear. I hadn't in the office and I wouldn't here. Wherever here was. Without lowering my guard or changing my expression, I tore my focus off him and scanned the room.

Sparse décor adorned the studio. Calling it an apartment seemed like a reach. At the bare minimum, this place could be inhabited, but it didn't resemble a well-lived-in home. A simple kitchenette faced me from the opposite wall, and the only other interior door led to a bathroom. The shower stall was visible from where I sat on this bed, but what gripped me the most was the bloody washcloth hanging from the rim of the tub.

He cleaned my wound. That gauze hadn't wrapped around my arm on its own. Alek must have done that too. His... care should've been touching. I should've felt better that he was motivated to see to my injury. But he'd caused it. Perhaps he hadn't shot me himself, but he'd instigated the situation where I was caught in gunfire.

No one else was here. It was only me and him, and I didn't know how this private isolation would fare for me.

"What the hell is going on?" I demanded as he stood near the bed.

He didn't reply, simply staring down at me like he wasn't sure what to do. All the power was in his hands. It wasn't just this submissive position, me seated on the bed and wounded. His presence screamed authority, but I didn't find comfort in it.

"I shouldn't be here."

He huffed, and I couldn't tell whether that was a sound of agreement or dark amusement. I risked a glance around him, wondering if I could run. That door would lead to my freedom, but I had no means to outrun him or escape his grasp. Looming over me like this, he damn well caged me in place.

"Did you hear me? I shouldn't be here. You've got no right bringing me here."

He shrugged.

I fumed, pissed off even more that he couldn't reply. He was just like all the other men I'd ever met in my life, in charge and never feeling the need to answer to a woman.

I refused to cave and let him see how much this silent treatment wore on me. I was tired. I was scared deep down, but most of all, my nerves were frayed beyond repair with this constant battery of stress.

"You need to take me back."

He huffed. "To your wedding?" His lips curled in a devilish smirk.

I doubted the church was left in any state to resume that ceremony. "To my father." Sitting up straighter, I tried to show how confident I was behind my words. "You're a dead man walking, capturing me at my wedding like that."

His shoulder shifted a bit in an indifferent shrug. "We're all one day closer to death anyway."

Morbid. I refused to let his devil-may-care attitude get to me. "I *knew* you were trouble the moment I saw you."

"Likewise." He paired that parroted reply with a long, lazy, and appreciative stare over me. From my cleavage to my eyes, he looked his fill, smiling that sinister smile of pure arrogance. I struggled to banish the thought that he was the predator closing in on his prey—me.

He didn't glance away. His hot, lustful focus remained on me. The longer he looked, the less he spoke. The air grew heavier and taut with this sparking pulse of awareness. It was stupid, but instinct kicked in. I wanted to know what he thought of what he saw, to know what he was even searching for. All I could guess was that his seductive expression wouldn't bode well for me. I grew uneasy, so openly studied like this by his intense eyes.

"Then you'd better take me back right now," I snapped, riled up from his gaze on me.

"Oh, I'd better, huh?" He smirked, stepping closer.

I fought not to tense up. I wouldn't show him fear or... anything else. This closer proximity pushed me to lash out again, at least verbally.

"He'll kill you. My father's men will not let this go. No corner of the city will keep you safe."

He rolled his eyes.

"I'm warning you, you'd better—"

He lifted his hand and snapped. Like I was a goddamn dog. "Shut up."

"No. You can't tell me to shut up and expect me to listen."

In a swift dip, he lowered toward me. Setting his hands on the bed, he forced me to retreat and lean backward, caged in by his thick arms, his fists on either side of my thighs. Breathing hard, I stared up at him and tensed. That pulse of awareness increased, and I damn near panted this close to his firm lips.

"Shut. Up." He tracked his dark stare from my eyes to my lips.

I tilted my head to the side and smirked. "No." As a matter of fact, a good scream was well past due. If anyone waited nearby, they'd hear me. I had to try. I sucked in a deep breath, preparing to give it my all.

"You'd better—"

He lunged forward, silencing my threat. His lips slammed over mine. With them already parted, he had full access to invade and plunder. His hot tongue speared in to duel with mine, and as he leaned down, pushing me, he dominated my first kiss.

I'd read about it in those old romance novels others left lying around. I'd seen movies. I understood the dynamics of kissing, but under Alek's rough touch, his hungry lips, I felt like an ignorant fool, glad to learn how this actually worked.

He brushed his lips over mine in a hard sweep, and the rub only enticed me to want it again. I gasped, reaching up to chase the thrill of his mouth on mine, his tongue tasting me, his hot breaths mixed with mine.

This brute was my enemy. He'd kidnapped me. He'd crashed my wedding and happily caused war.

But none of that could matter. Not one of those facts entered my mind as I succumbed to his addictive, spicy taste. I didn't think about anything but the seductive pull of wanting more. A harder kiss. A longer sample. I moaned, overwhelmed with this eagerness to pull him down and never let go.

He loomed so big and powerful, masculine and larger than life. With this kiss, he demanded that I try to match him. He growled and lifted his hand to hold the back of my head. His fingers slipped through my hair, and with his punishing grip, he angled me right where he wanted me as he kissed me silent.

I'd never experienced this consuming desire, lit to flaming within seconds. Even as it rocked me to my core, a thread of common sense prevailed. In a fit of reclaiming my mind and ignoring how he made me feel, I bit his lip.

He parted, hissing then licking the bite mark I'd given him. Through narrowed eyes, he glared at me, darker and angrier than before since I'd retaliated.

My God. What am I doing? As I panted and glowered right back at him, I warred with wanting his lips back where they were. Mine were moist, cooling in the air, and I slammed them shut and scowled. "How dare you take what's not yours!"

His reply wasn't what I expected. He arched one brow, giving me a dark look. If I could try to guess and read his mind, he was wondering if he *should* take me. He confirmed it with just as many filthy, smug words. "I've got you here. Why not?"

My nipples beaded and my pussy clenched. Just the mere idea of this man taking me however he pleased... It turned me on. He didn't retreat, nor did he lunge forward. Licking his lip and studying me with so much heat, he paused.

He didn't look at me like Geoff had. Andrey's lewd glances weren't like Alek's smoldering gaze of pure seduction. Alek regarded me like I was a woman he craved, and it was a heady sensation to manage.

Me. This rugged, sexy man wanted *me.*

"Why not?" I snapped. There were so many reasons. At the top of that list was the fact that I wasn't his. I wasn't Alek's woman to have. But nowhere in my mind did I cling to the argument that I didn't want him.

Because against everything warning me otherwise, I did.

"Because I'm not worth it."

His eyebrows dipped in a harsh slant as he focused on me. "What do you mean?"

Still, he caged me, his strong arms bracketing me to the bed, but he'd lost some of that seductive air. I'd distracted him with my words, and that was exactly what I needed. I should be distracting him so I could evade him and run.

"You could find something better than this." I gestured my trembling hand at my body. I didn't fear him. Not out of a worry of physical pain. So far, he wanted to keep me alive and well. But I'd never played a game like this before, a twist of words and flirty advances.

"You could find a skinnier woman. Someone prettier." I said it to reject him, to dissuade him, but the words came so easily. I'd spent all my life hearing that kind of criticism from my father. It wasn't hard to claim that I was less than.

"Why would I want that?" He trailed his hand from the back of my head down along my neck. Every touch of the back of his knuckles over my flesh felt like a delicate caress that lit me up inside, feather-light and too tender. He dragged my focus from his face as I watched him trace his fingers along the neckline of my dress.

Mere inches were left between his fingers and my breasts. Just seeing him this close and almost to my nipples threw me off balance. My breath hitched, and I froze, watching and wishing he'd push the fabric down.

"Skinnier?" he retorted sarcastically. He stroked his fingers over the side of my breast, teasing me with that faint contact. "No. Skin and bones don't appeal."

I gulped, stuck between the urge to reach up and kiss him and breathing quickly enough.

"Prettier?" He growled softly, leaning in to nuzzle the side of my face. From my jaw to my ear, he dragged his nose and inhaled deeply. His lips brushed up my cheek with the motion, and I closed my eyes at the tickle of what he promised.

"Fuck pretty." He kissed just below my ear. "You're *gorgeous*."

I shivered.

He brought his hand back up to trace along my neckline. "Sexy," he added, kissing that sensitive spot beneath my ear again.

One fingertip edged beneath the fabric of my dress, and I let out a whine of need.

"And right now, you're mine to do whatever I want with."

Fuck that! His dominant touch was frying my senses, but hearing his cocky claim jolted me. I reared back. "Fuck off." As I tried to take advantage of the distraction, I leaned to the side. I didn't slip away far. He was too quick. He hadn't lowered his guard, not at all, it seemed. His thick arm wrapped around my waist as he hauled me back to the bed.

Unlike the scene at the church, I could fight back here. I flailed and wrestled, punching and kicking for all I had. In the end, after the short scrimmage, he proved he was stronger, faster, and more determined.

Rope dug into my wrists with the bindings he'd strung there. Over my mouth rested a slim strip of fabric he'd ripped from my wedding dress. Ribbons weren't supposed to be gags, but Alek was resourceful enough to use whatever was on hand.

Tied to the bed frame, muted with a gag, I fumed and glared at him, praying he could see the hatred in my eyes. If he did, he didn't show it. Instead, as I screamed my frustration in my mind, he stood and brushed off his shirt, fixing himself from the scuffle.

"You're not going anywhere, Mila. The faster you come to terms with that, the better."

Another man telling me what to do. I was sick of it. And I vowed to never obey a single damn thing he said.

11

ALEK

She sat there glowering and fuming. Her cheeks were pink when I kissed her, but now, as she eyed me with such beautiful fury, she was ravishing. That blush deepened with anger. Those bold blue eyes radiated with such fire. She was breathtaking, alive with this rage.

Fuck, is she something else.

I couldn't remember a time I'd ever been so drawn to, so mercilessly hungry for a woman. No one compared. But I knew better than to try to get closer. She couldn't hurt me. That gag prevented her from biting me, and with her hands bound to the headboard, she wouldn't get far in attacking me. Mila wasn't going anywhere, and the only good option that remained for me was to let her stew and simmer.

She could hate me as much as she wanted, but only if she could admit why. Sure, she was pissed. I expected that much. I had kidnapped her, after all. But she'd be a liar if she told me she was upset to miss out on marrying Andrey. If I hadn't been watching her so closely, I would've missed the slight glance to the side she did when I challenged her.

When I asked if she wanted me to take her back to that wedding, she couldn't reply in the affirmative.

Because she hadn't wanted to get stuck with him. She hadn't wanted to marry him. I'd done her a fucking favor getting her out of there, and until she could agree with me on that point, I didn't want to waste my breath.

She fidgeted, testing the bindings at her wrists. After she pulled and tugged, grunting at the effort to wrestle out of the secure grips, she winced and dipped her face to look at her arm.

"Don't fight it." I stepped back to the bed, chancing this proximity to examine her arm again. If she resisted and kept at this, she'd only worsen that wound. Her shoulder tensed as I grabbed her arm and lifted it to see the gauze. As she wriggled to wrench out of my hold, I grinned.

Sassy, stubborn little fighter.

The fabric was still white, not pink or red with new bleeding, and I felt good about her injury. She was awake, no longer worrying me about her state of consciousness. She was alert and not in pain—

Her stomach growled.

I eyed her sternly, debating the wisdom of taking that gag off. "Behave."

She furrowed her brows as I stepped away.

I returned with a water bottle and a plate of crackers and dried fruit, simple non-perishables I'd found in the cabinets. "Behave or this goes back on."

Her gorgeous stare stayed on me the entire time I loosened the gag and let it drop to her neck. As she worked her mouth open and closed and licked her plump lips, she said, "How am I supposed to feed myself?"

I didn't reply, loosening her hands so that they remained connected to the headboard but with enough slack that she could eat and drink. She wasn't going anywhere. Even though I compromised to see to her nourishment, I was no fool. That faint glimmer of hope in her eyes wouldn't get her far. She didn't wait, taking the water first. I watched as she snacked, never lowering her scowl from me.

After one last look over her, committing her furious expression to memory, I turned to pace at the other side of the room while she ate.

Distance helped. She was a force. A magnet. And fuck it, she was a distraction I'd have to work hard at ignoring.

I had no business kissing her. I didn't have a reason to lean in and toy with her, to play with her and touch her the little that I had. Those touches were mere examples of what I wanted. If I'd had the time and freedom to give in to my desires, I would've had my hands full of her luscious tits and sweet curves.

It was time to do damage control. I'd instigated the damage, and I stood by it, but I had to check in and see what I could do about steering it. First, I called my brothers. Maxim and Dmitri didn't answer, but I refused to worry. They were instructed to be careful and hide, and they damn well better have done just that.

As I called Ivan and waited for him to answer, my phone beeped with an incoming text. The message was short and to the point, as was Nik's style.

Nikolai: *I'm coming over.*

I didn't need to worry about his trip here. He was too smart to be tailed, and I wondered how far away he might be. I didn't have to wait long. Before I could start redialing Ivan, since he hadn't answered when I thought he would, two succinct raps sounded on the door.

It was Nik's signature knock, and I let him in. Nothing could have prepared me for how bad he could've looked, but he didn't give me a chance to fuss over him.

"Fuck," I said on an angry exhale.

He pushed right past me, leaving me to close and lock the door after him as he headed toward the bathroom. On the way there, his head turned slightly as he noticed Mila sitting on the bed. She still snacked, glowering with every bite.

"Ivan looks worse," Nikolai said as he turned the faucet on and began to wet his bloody hands.

"Pavel did this?" I wasn't shocked that he'd want to come after my brothers for how I'd stopped Andrey's wedding. Our uncle would want blood. I knew this. But seeing my sibling beaten and bloody filled me with an instant, ugly rage.

Nik nodded. "Well, Andrey wouldn't get his hands dirty and do it himself." He wet another washcloth and began clearing the blood from his face. "Had Igor do it. And Stephan. Ivan was taken to the warehouse." Pausing to look at my reflection in the mirror, he raised his brows. "He won't talk."

I sighed, dipping my head in a slight nod. If I spoke, I'd scream. My brothers were no weaklings. They could take a hit or two, but I still hated that my actions were impacting them the most so far.

"Maxim and Dmitri are sticking together," he said. "Pavel wants blood. *Your* blood."

No shit.

"Any of the men he even thinks of as a traitor, anyone he assumes is a supporter, he's pulled in to question." He wet the rag again and continued wiping at his face. "He's not going to kill us. Too valuable for information."

I shook my head and offered him a towel to dry off the wounds. Now that the blood was cleared away, it didn't look that bad. Maybe he was right. Pavel wanted to keep them all alive to beat them again. It wouldn't matter. My brothers wouldn't fess up. They'd protect me. If I could avoid more pain on their shoulders, though, I would.

"Kastava is threatening war," he added quieter, leaning around me to glance in the direction of the bed where Mila sat. This studio apartment didn't offer much for privacy. Whatever he said, she'd likely hear.

He slanted toward me and sighed. "Kastava vows to end the Valkov Bratva."

"He won't," I argued just as quietly. My Family would not be done away with, not like this. All I wanted was to secure my Family, not ruin it. Preventing an alliance with our enemies was the only way to go about making it happen.

"We will be stronger. Without them," I swore. "I will rebuild stronger in a way we never could have with them trying to get into our business."

His nod was a weak reply, but I didn't need to remind him about what was at stake. I followed him out of the bathroom, watching as he got a water bottle out of the fridge. Once more, he glanced at Mila. He drank the water and considered her snacking in mulish silence. He seemed curious but knew better than to speak to her.

"How?" he asked me. "How can we start the process of rebuilding stronger? While Pavel is mad and focusing on finding you and making you pay, what can we do?"

I shoved my hands in my pockets and exhaled a long, hard breath. "We get answers. Meet up with Ivan and go down to the docks again. Investigate this big shipment." I'd already texted them all what I'd overheard before the wedding. "Check out the office. Find evidence that Pavel can't ignore. Or find someone who can explain those codes."

Nik rubbed his jaw, nodding. "They have to reference a third party."

I agreed. "Someone else who is helping the Kastavas try to fuck us over."

He left, in a hurry to help however he could while everyone would be up in arms about how I'd crashed the wedding. I hated to feel like I was hiding from the action, but I knew that staying here and keeping this bride out of the equation was my role.

After he was gone, I returned to her, finding her still pissed and scowling. The plate was empty, as was the water bottle.

"Want more?" I offered.

She tilted her head to the side. "More of…?"

I pointed at the plate and bottle. "Did you have enough?"

She didn't reply, lowering her gaze and licking her lips. "No," she murmured softly.

"What do you want?" I asked, ready to get another water bottle.

"What do I want?" She gazed up at me with hooded eyes, so obvious with her coy and sultry look.

Oh. I see how it is. While I could appreciate her attempts to tease me, she had a lesson to learn. It would take a *lot* more than that to manipulate me. I wasn't mad, though, but amused. If she thought she could trick me, acting all sexy and acting innocent like this, she really was naïve. Ignorant. It again reminded me of how young she was. A young lady, not an experienced woman who knew how to play with a man like me. And it would be too much fun to play with her and show her how this worked.

"Yeah." I leaned in until she fell back on the bed. Covering her with my body, I braced myself on my forearms, relishing every sweet press of her soft body beneath mine, all those sexy, soft curves, every push of her breasts against my chest. "What do you want?"

"I..." She frowned, her eyes wider with alarm as she adjusted to our position. Her arms remained tied, and with the quickness of how I'd covered her on the bed, the bindings twisted and trapped her hands over her head.

"I..."

I kissed away her indecision, and within a moment of her soft lips parting under mine, I had her mewling and gasping for more.

"You want some comfort?" I taunted, reaching beneath her torn dress. Her panties were nothing but a thin scrap of satin, a thong that easily ripped in my grip.

"Alek!"

Oh, fuck. She'd shouted it in shock, but hearing her say my name was something wicked and sweet. I'd have her screaming it in no time.

I covered her mouth with mine again, kissing her deeply. I stole her breaths and forced her lips apart wider as I tasted her. She didn't hesitate to reply in kind.

Just like that. She melted in my arms, arching toward me and eager for my touch. Under her dress, I stroked my finger back and forth along her slit until I slipped two fingers into her soaked pussy. Dripping. She was so wet with arousal that I knew this had to be her first time. She was too tight, too impatient.

"Can't you—" She gasped as I pumped my fingers into her faster. "Can't you untie me?"

"Why the fuck would I do that?"

"So I can—" She sucked in a hard breath as I added another finger. Her moan was the filthiest, sexiest sound.

"So I can touch you too."

I kissed her quiet, fingering her faster and getting her off all too easily. She was definitely a virgin, coming so fast like that. Her pussy clenched my digits, and as her cream slickened and dripped, smeared over her thighs as I removed my fingers, I kept my eyes on her face.

Her brow remained furrowed, her eyes shut tight. She panted and strained to catch her breath, but soon enough, she wrenched her eyes open and stared up at me. "I want... I want to touch you too."

I scoffed, getting off the bed and ignoring how hard I was from getting her off.

"Alek. No. Come back. Let me touch you."

"So you can run?" I shook my head. "I'm not that fucking stupid."

"Alek," she growled, tugging her hands and trying to get out. "Just let me—"

I yanked her gag back up and secured it, reducing her to mad, muffled mumbles. Kneeling on the bed as I tightened her hands toward the headboard, I made eye contact once more. "I'm not letting you go until I'm ready."

12

MILA

I woke up the next morning still tied to the headboard. He'd left me enough slack that I could bring my hands down to sleep with them at my chest, but he hadn't budged an inch about removing my gag.

He'd untied me in the evening so I could go to the restroom, but he gave no indication of letting me talk. Instead of fighting the point, I eventually gave in to sleep. My body was simply too tired to stay up. I hadn't slept the night before the wedding. I'd been running on fumes, charged with stress. Between his letting me have food and water, then...

I squeezed my eyes closed at the memory of him playing with me. His rough fingers touching me where no other man ever had, his mouth demanding my kisses as he fingered me so expertly. I'd never come for a man before. Only myself. And damn, what a difference it was. Shame hit me, but it didn't last long. I should've been humiliated that he'd gotten me off so quickly. I should've been furious that my kidnapper thought he had any right to touch me so intimately.

More than anything, though, I should've been livid that he manipulated me in *my* attempt to trick *him*. He was no stupid soldier, young and clueless when a woman was within reach. Alek was an older, wiser man, and that was what irked me most. He'd humored me, seeing through my attempt to con him into untying me. *Of course*, it couldn't have been that simple. Still, I'd tried. I couldn't just give in. I had to keep my head up and fight for a way out of this predicament.

I turned my head on the bed, finding him still asleep. We were both fully clothed. He still wore his suit, minus the jacket and shoes. My bloody, ripped wedding gown still covered my body.

Minus my panties. I glowered at the ceiling.

He'd lain next to me without touching me. It was probably another way of keeping tabs on me. If I so much as fidgeted, the mattress would give my actions away.

While he slept, I considered my options. That was a pragmatic approach to what I could do next. Thinking about his kisses and how he unabashedly got me off like that… Those thoughts wouldn't do me any good.

I was stuck here. I couldn't run, not while I was tied up, and he'd made it clear that he had no intention of untying me.

I couldn't call for help. I had no phone. Nothing. Even if I had a phone, I wouldn't have known what to say. I didn't know where this crummy apartment was in the city. Or if it even was in the city anymore.

Rescue didn't seem like a reality I could count on, but I had to admit it wasn't necessary. On a simple basis, I didn't *need* to be rescued. I wasn't in harm's way. I had to believe that Alek wouldn't seriously hurt me. He was rough when he kissed me and filthily demanding when he played with my pussy. These scraps of fabric weren't comfortable around my wrists. But he was taking care of me.

In more ways than one...

I rolled my eyes at the ceiling, still thrown off at how easily he'd made me come and how... good it was. I'd practically passed out from the euphoria of that release, and I hated that he'd done it. If I were to ever find a man to be intimate with, I'd want—

What am I saying? What I want? I'd never had a chance to actually think I could have what *I* wanted. I was a pawn and always would be.

Alek hadn't been cruel, though. He saw to my pleasure. It had been on his terms. I didn't have a chance to stop him, but—

Oh, just stop thinking about it already!

I knew if Geoff or Andrey—or any other man—had me tied up and at their disposal, they would have shown no mercy. Alek wasn't upfront with what he did want from me, and it felt like I was due an answer.

Wriggling my lips, I loosened my gag until I could push it away from my lips. My tongue felt fuzzy and dry, both from fighting the gag and with the need for water.

"Alek."

He didn't stir, and I almost found it comical that he could sleep that soundly and deeply.

I turned the other way, glancing at the clock. I'd never slept in this late, and I despised that this time with Alek was feeling a lot like freedom. I was bound, but he was generous in ways he couldn't understand.

He gave me food without question, unlike the strict diet I'd faced at home.

He let me come in his hand without expecting anything in return, unlike my greatest fears of what I'd encounter as Andrey's wife.

He allowed me to sleep in, with no demands to get up and serve him.

"Alek." I twisted my hips and kneed his thigh. That did the trick. He stirred, rubbing his face as he scowled at me.

"What?" He glanced at my gag hanging loose under my chin.

"I want to talk."

He rolled his eyes and sat up. "Then talk."

I opened my mouth but he cut me off.

"Don't waste your time asking to be released."

I shut my mouth and sighed. We entered another stare-down and I wished for a witty comeback. Nothing came to me, and he raised his brows in silent question. I hated that my silence was basically an admission that he was in charge. But literally nothing came to me. I didn't know what to say. "I meant I wanted *you* to talk."

He grinned, dark and slow. "Because you're deluded enough to think *you're* in charge here?"

I didn't respond, depriving him of the satisfaction.

If he didn't want to kill me, he had to realize I was more worthy alive. And if he wanted me alive, I had to serve some kind of purpose. His act of kidnapping me had to be a step toward stopping the Valkov-Kastava union, but why? Whatever his reasoning, I wouldn't fight it.

"I'll help you." I blurted it out too quickly, and he didn't seem to be swayed by my offer. "What do you want?"

"From you?" He smirked. "I don't trust you."

"It's not like I tied you up and kidnapped anyone. I'm the trustworthy one between the two of us!"

"You're a Kastava."

"And you're a Valkov." We were enemies and we knew it. "Or you *were*."

He paused in sliding his legs off the bed to glower over his shoulder at me.

"Why are you defying your Family?" I'd heard his brother yesterday, how Pavel Valkov was out to get him now. Blurred memories of the church stayed in my mind, and I recalled how all the men shouted at him to stop. Alek had caused war by intervening at my wedding. He'd risked his family's wrath in doing so.

"I'm not defying my Family." He stood and walked toward the kitchenette.

"You are!" I protested, watching him grab some things and set them on a plate. "Your uncle isn't pleased with you."

Neither is my father.

He didn't reply, preparing a couple of plates of simple foods. With a couple of water bottles tucked under his arm, he returned and shoved one plate toward me.

"Alek, why—"

He shot me a stern look to shut up and I huffed out a breath. I accepted the plate, pleased that he didn't skimp on the offerings. Crackers, cheese, nuts, and more dried fruit. It was the biggest meal I'd had all year.

Before he started on his food, he checked my wound. He uncoiled a bit of the gauze and checked that it wasn't inflamed, then wrapped it back up.

I couldn't make sense of him. He wanted me fed and well. Healthy and uninjured. I didn't know enough about him, but I understood that he was a hard man. He wasn't doting on me, but... something else.

Is he keeping me in good health because I need to be in good condition when he returns me to my father? The thought of that future didn't fill me with comfort. I swallowed a bite and watched him pick up his plate. "Are you going to deliver me back to my father?"

He didn't speak. His mouth was full of food as he peered at me dully, but his dry expression spoke volumes. As we ate, he didn't tell me a single detail about any of his plans. "War was inevitable," he stated instead. It was a cryptic reply, but I would take it for what it was worth—stupidity.

"Not before you burst into my wedding like that."

He shook his head. "Our families cannot align. Not like they wanted it to. Therefore, war was inevitable, and change will follow."

For the better or worse, though?

"You broke your Family's loyalty, striking against the wishes of the rightful head of your bratva."

He scoffed. "Spoken like a properly trained bratva woman, huh?"

"It's true. You've ruined the loyalty by disobeying your—"

His plate slid on his lap as he abruptly lowered it. "Ruined the loyalty? No, I fucking did not. And I've never felt that my uncle was a leader in any sense of the word."

I blinked, digesting his words. This was a huge comment to share, a significant opinion. No one—and I meant no one—ever dared to speak against their Pakhan like that.

He noticed how quiet I became, but I couldn't break out of my stunned stupor over what he'd admitted.

"You're going rogue, then?" I guessed carefully.

"No." His denial was calm and quick. "I'm not going rogue. I'm not going anywhere. It's the other way around. My Family, the Valkov Bratva, has been letting *me* down. Pavel and Andrey have been disappointing many of my brothers. They are too blind to see what is happening, high on power." He faced me, cool and confident as he explained. "My uncle and cousin were oblivious to the fact that *your* Family wants to take us over."

I opened and closed my mouth, put on the spot to reply to that claim.

"I suspected from the beginning that the Kastavas want to take over." He held my stare, tipping his chin up a bit. That direct gaze pinned me, and I felt on edge being under pressure like this. Why did I ever open my damn mouth and want to talk to this man?

"Can you deny it?" he demanded.

"No." My response left my lips before I could call it back. It was the truth, but I couldn't support it. I couldn't back it up with any evidence or reasons. It simply made sense. Sergei Kastava was a greedy, power-hungry man. He seldom considered stopping at anything. The fact that he'd ordered me to report to him after I married Andrey was another example of his coveting and clinging to any semblance of power he saw.

As I went quiet, preferring this silence over speaking, I felt his eyes on me. Alek's attention was a tangible caress, heated and steady, like a physical touch.

He wanted to know more. I couldn't agree with him that my family had nefarious plans with his family and not say anything else. He had to be burning with curiosity, and he would soon pair that with orders to explain.

But I couldn't. I had never been privy to any important information. I was ignorant of any big plans to take over another rival, but I knew that the simple statement of a takeover would make sense.

I met his gaze and cringed. His grin didn't welcome me to feel confident. Again, I convinced myself that I was the prey and he was the predator. Because he watched me with a sinful excitement, eager to lord his power over me once more.

"Maybe you had a good idea there."

I arched my brow, not trusting his mischievous smile as he took our plates and set them on a table. "What…" I cleared my throat and tried speaking again. "What do you mean?"

"You said you wanted to talk," he reminded me as he returned to the bed, standing over me, so helpless and bound. "So, let's see about you giving me some answers."

Oh, shit. I gulped, nervous more than ever.

13

ALEK

She lowered her gaze, pressing her lips in a firm line.

Ah. Not so chatty now, are you?

I tipped her chin up and kept my two fingers right there. They waited so close to her neck, and I battled the urge to stroke my hand down it and hold on. Touching her was becoming an addiction, and I wasn't above using this contact to get my way with her.

"You agree that your father wants to take over my family."

She exhaled a shaky breath and glared at me. "I won't repeat myself. You heard me the first time."

I chewed on my lip, fighting a smile. She was so fucking bold, never afraid to talk back. It fueled my desire like nothing else.

"Starting with your marriage to my cousin."

She shrugged, and I narrowed my eyes at her reaction.

"Is that false?"

"I don't know. I…" She hesitated, breathing evenly before lifting her blue gaze to me again. "I don't know anything about my marriage. Why it was decided the way it was."

"Cut the bullshit."

"I don't! I only learned that I was to be Andrey's bride three days before the wedding. My father—No. He wasn't the one to even break the news. I found out from another woman within the bratva. She overheard the men talking about it, and it wasn't until that evening that he bothered to inform me that I was being married off."

I lowered to the bed, sitting next to her as she struggled to sit up. Her bound hands prevented her from accomplishing any upright position, though, and I wasn't inclined to help her. She could try to bolt again.

"I've always known I would be arranged in a marriage someday."

I peered at her, intrigued about her tone and her choice of words. "Why do you say it like that?"

She licked her lips, seeming bothered to speak up about it. "I… My father has always criticized me. He's told me many times that he would struggle to find a man who would want me for a bride. He implied that offering me to a man would be an insult."

Ah. Her comments from yesterday were starting to make sense. Sergei Kastava had filled his daughter's head with lies and garbage, but she wasn't fooling me. Mila knew her worth. She appreciated her body and had taken care to work what she had. I saw it in that office, when she wore such sex kitten clothes tailored just to suit her delectable curves.

"Why does this marriage matter so much?"

She furrowed her brows, staring at me like *I* was the one who'd know the answer to that. Pavel preached that Andrey and Mila's marriage would unify our bratvas. That with them joined as a couple, the families could no longer be enemies. I was convinced something else had to be at play.

"I... I don't know what you mean." She shrugged again, and I was distracted with a loose, wavy strand of her hair tumbling over her bare shoulder.

"What do the Kastavas stand to gain with your marrying Andrey?"

She smirked, letting a slow, naughty smile curve her lips. "Well, I *didn't* marry him, did I?"

I deadpanned, not in the mood to join in her sarcasm.

Shaking her head slightly, she tried to get more comfortable with her bound hands. "I'm not sure what you're asking. And I'm not sure how to answer that. I assumed marrying Andrey would just be a way to align our families and unite us all. But..." She sighed, frowning once more.

"But what?"

She worked her mouth open and closed, struggling to know what to say as she seemed to search for words. "But my father has never been one to..."

What are you hiding? Out with it.

"Be a team player. He's not even that dedicated to keeping *our* family united. He cuts his losses easily, and I truly can't understand why he would want to align with another bratva. Especially a larger one that's been around far longer than ours."

I watched her, studying her closely for a tell. That strange feeling was back. My gut was warning me that she wasn't being completely honest, and I loathed how uneasy it made me feel. It would be stupid to think that I *wanted* to trust her. I couldn't. I never would, and it was a sign of my own weakness that I wanted her confidence.

"What else?"

She shrugged. "Nothing. That's all I can think of."

"What are you hiding?"

She rolled her eyes. "Nothing."

Despite her insistence, I couldn't shake that nagging suspicion, just like what I felt when I saw her at that shipping office. She was no fool.

"I'm certain it's no different in the Valkov Bratva." She huffed, looking away for a moment. "Bratva women are to please their men. We aren't included in things that matter, like making decisions or contributing to plans. I know nothing."

"Even though you are his daughter?"

Her hair fell out of the last of that braided knot with her nod. "He didn't trust me."

Neither will I.

"He trusted you to run that office where I met you."

"Barely. It's just a front, a company to make it look legit."

"And you still want to claim that you're ignorant of why you were expected to marry Andrey?"

She nodded.

"And you want to insist that you know nothing about that big shipment coming up? The trade that is supposed to mark the beginning of the Valkovs and the Kastavas as allies?"

This time, she wasn't so quick to nod.

I watched her swallow and glance away for the barest moment. "No. I know nothing, Alek. I was never trusted."

I don't believe you. I refused to think she was coming completely clean, but I wouldn't hold it against her. I already knew she was feisty and strong. All that meant was that I'd need to try another way to get the truth out of her.

"Never trusted, huh?" I twisted, reaching her wrists where they were still bound. "I guess I'm no different."

She glowered at me as I dragged my fingers down her arm, teasing her skin with a delicate touch.

"No. All you men are exactly the same."

I kept my hand on her, lowering it over her shoulder and moving toward her breast. Her breathing increased in tempo, and her eyes lost some of that sass. Something like desire lit them now.

"You want to compare me to your groom?" I taunted.

She parted her lips to reply, but she never spoke. A sweet gasp left her mouth instead as I tugged her dress down and revealed her breasts. The generous swell of her tit spilled out, and I latched my gaze on her nipple. "Fuck." She was exquisite. So smooth, so curvy. All ripe, and mine for the taking.

"Alek." She uttered it on a breathy exhale as I cupped her globe, taunting her with a hard squeeze.

I leaned down to kiss her at the same time I yanked on her gown again. As her other breast was exposed, I closed my mouth over hers and stole a deep, rough kiss.

"Marrying a man like Andrey isn't what you would have wanted," I warned against her kiss-swollen lips.

She blinked at me, panting and alert with lust. "You..." She shook her head slightly. "You can't begin to know what I want."

"No?" I kissed her again, thrilled when she growled into my mouth and sucked on my tongue. But I didn't linger. Keeping one hand on her tit, I left her mouth and trailed kisses along her neck, intent on proving her wrong.

"You need a strong man." I sucked on her neck as I rolled her nipple between my finger and thumb.

She huffed a single laugh. "You mean one who won't hide behind me in gunfire?"

I continued down, kissing along her collarbone, leading toward her breasts. At the first touch of my lips on her sweet globes, she cried out and arched toward me. I laved and licked, then sucked and nipped. Between her breasts, I paid equal attention with my hand, mouth, and tongue. Only when she was panting and writhing, pushing her chest up to me, did I stop.

"You need a man who can handle you and appreciate your fire."

She blinked, looking lost in a mix of surprise and desire. Perhaps she wasn't used to compliments, and she should take that as one. As I sat up, she pouted until she caught herself. "I..." She glanced at her bare breasts, then my mouth. "I—"

"You want a man who can give you what you need." I knew she wouldn't last. She was too impatient. I had her right where I wanted her, horny and on edge for more.

"I..." She growled as I stared at the wet peaks of her nipples. "I sure don't want you."

"I bet I can prove you wrong." I returned to her breasts, sucking and biting harder. Once more, she mewled and cried out, so loud and eager to contradict herself. As she pushed her tits at my mouth, I yanked her dress up.

"What are you hiding?" I demanded again.

"Wha—" She tried to sit up as I crawled further from her breasts. "What?"

"I know you're hiding something."

"I... no."

I tugged harder at her dress, annoyed with the billowing layers that prevented me from seeing her face as I lowered mine toward her sweet pussy. Liar. She could tell me that she didn't want me, but her body betrayed her. I saw the truth in her glistening folds. She was dripping, soaked with her cream for me. Without bringing my lips to her succulent flesh, I stayed close so she could feel the whips of air from my exhales. Slowly and steadily, I pumped my fingers into her hot slickness.

So tight. So wet. She was perfection, and with a carnal glee, I knew that I would be the first to ever sample her.

"What are you hiding?"

She dropped her head back, groaning. "Nothing!"

"Really?" I added another finger and pumped faster.

"Yes!"

I paused, earning her grunt of protest. "You want me to keep going?"

"I…" She lifted her head to glower at me.

I grinned, knowing she wouldn't say it. She hated me too much, and I knew she loathed how I was proving her wrong. She didn't just want me. She needed me.

"You tell me what you're hiding." I pulled my fingers out so I could hold her folds wide open. A quick push on her thigh made her legs part open wider, and I pressed my tongue to her cream-coated skin.

"Oh, fuck. Oh, my—Oh, fuck."

She dropped her other leg to the opposite side, and I dragged my tongue over her sensitive flesh. From her entrance all the way up to her clit, I stroked and tasted her sweet tanginess.

"You tell me what you're hiding and I'll keep going," I explained before I went faster. I left no spot untouched. I swiped my tongue along her folds, speared it into her entrance, and circled her hard little clit. Once she seemed close, thrusting her hips to my face and making the sexiest moans, I stopped.

She cried out, cringing at me as I lifted my head and looked at her. Air cooled the cream that clung to my chin, but I let her see it, proving how aroused she was. If I wasn't mistaken, this was likely her first time with this, and I could drag it out all fucking night.

"No!"

"Tell me what you're hiding."

"I'm not hiding anything! No one ever trusted me with any information!"

I returned my fingers to her pussy, slipping two in to piston hard and fast. Within another moment, she was on the verge of coming again. "I don't believe you."

"I—Oh! I don't know anything."

Again, I stopped. This constant halting was gnawing on me. Every time she gave me those sexy sounds and each time I felt her legs quivering with her pending orgasm, my dick got harder and harder. I was torturing her as I withheld orgasms, but it was driving me hotter too.

"Alek!"

"You wanna come?"

"I—Yes!" She gripped her bindings and pushed her pussy toward me.

"Then tell me the truth."

"I did. I will."

I narrowed my eyes. That sounded like a fucking contradiction. She could swear that she *had* told me the truth in the same breath that she would agree to yet?

"Whatever you ask me," she got out around harsh breaths, "I'll tell you the truth. Please."

Her sobs turned me on to the point of no return, and I felt like we'd come to enough of an understanding. Besides, I couldn't last long myself. With her sweet scent heavy in the air, her cream on my tongue, I needed to fuck her before I shot my cum into my pants.

"No going back on that, Mila. You hear me?"

I unzipped my pants, needing to stroke my dick to relieve the pressure as I dropped my mouth back to her pussy.

"Yes. I hear you—Oh!" She bucked at my suction on her clit. When I switched, rubbing her hard bud and eating at her pussy, she cried out an incoherent chant. I bet it killed her to beg for it, but I didn't care. As soon as I got her to come after that back and forth of preventing her from getting there, I was filling this tight cunt with my dick. I stroked my cock as I ate at her, and the second she came, squirting on my tongue slightly, I groaned right along with her.

"Alek!" she screamed. She fucking screamed my name, just like I knew she would, and I didn't stop. I chased her high, licking harder and faster and slurping at her cream as her orgasm left her shaking.

"I need, please, I want…" She was a mess of blubbering phrases, unable to string a sentence together as I leaned up and pumped my hand over my cock. "I want—" She locked her gaze on my dick, and I knelt closer, about to pop her cherry.

"You want this?" I held my dick up, triumphant that I'd proved her wrong. Fuck that nonsense about her not wanting me. She was feral for me.

Before I could line up my cock to her sweet pussy, a loud crash sounded in the room.

She screamed as the window burst in, and I dove to cover her.

1 4

MILA

My heart lurched into my throat, pounding hard as I struggled with another scream. Fear enveloped me. All traces of that bliss from my orgasm were gone. I was no longer turned on, eager and impatient for Alek to fill me with his long, hard cock.

Panic and utter fright. I was locked in a world of terror, trapped and tied to the bed with no means to run or hide or protect myself as the soldier rolled on the floor after breaking into the apartment. I hadn't paid much attention to the one window of this place. It was curtained so well that it blended into the bland details.

But one of my father's men had reached it. He'd broken in, and now as he skidded to a stop, he aimed a gun at us.

Alek plastered himself over me, and I wanted to sink into the mattress beneath him. Even if he hadn't tried to paint the differences between himself and every other man, I witnessed this critical difference in live action.

Andrey had used me as a shield. But Alek covered my body with his to shield *me*.

In the same deft dive he made to cover me, he reached to the side and pulled his gun from the holster on his back. He hadn't even gotten to the stage of taking his clothes off before he fucked me, and now I was glad for it.

He leaned over, his strong arm locked and strong as he aimed his gun.

Everything happened so quickly, it felt like a macabre blur, but I recognized the soldier. Yusef, one of my father's oldest, most trusted men. He rose up on one knee, leaving it among the shards of glass, to aim his gun right at me.

I squeezed my eyes shut and turned my face to Alek's shoulder as Yusef pulled the trigger. He fired faster. I felt the kickback from Alek's gun with his body smashed over mine, and I held my breath.

Another shot was fired, but I lived. No searing pain touched me, and Alek didn't grunt in pain either.

"You motherfucker!" Yusef roared, pulling my focus toward him. I opened my eyes and fought the instant urge to gag at the sight of his forearm as a mangled, bloody mess. Alek had aimed precisely at his gun hand and hadn't missed. Yusef's gun clattered to the floor, busting another piece of the glass.

Alek didn't speak as he rolled off me and stalked toward the intruder. I lifted and kicked my legs, trying to get my dress to fall over my bare pussy, but I couldn't hide my breasts with Alek no longer covering me. Modesty was overrated at the moment, though. I doubted Yusef cared as Alek fired twice more, getting the man in his knees.

Yusef toppled forward, right onto the glass, and I tensed at each vicious shout and groan that left his lips. Threats and curses, hexes and damns. He hurtled every profanity he could at Alek, but he didn't seem to listen as he tucked his dick back into his pants and zipped up. Keeping his gun at the ready, he approached Yusef then walked past him. As he walked across the room, he breathed hard, and his broad back rose and fell with his rapid inhales. It was another testament to his strength and athletic fitness. First, he went to the window and checked whether anyone else was coming. Then he slammed down a storm covering to close the entrance Yusef had formed.

I watched him, tense and so agitated from this sudden shock that I didn't know where else to look. Seeing that tall, strong man grounded me somehow, and I was afraid to take my eyes off him. Try as I might, I couldn't tune out Yusef's yelling and groaning. He remained on the floor, cut among the pieces of glass and Alek's precise shots.

Alek stood before him, training his gun on the bleeding man. Before he addressed him, he looked at me. "Are you all right?"

All right? Holy shit, no, I wasn't *all right*. I had just gone from the high of almost losing my virginity to my enemy to screaming for the fear of losing my life. Still, I nodded shakily and tried to steady my breaths.

I am all right. Because you protected me.

He nodded in reply, grabbing a towel from the back of a chair and tossing it to me. The room wasn't that large, so I wasn't shocked that he threw it with accuracy, covering my bare breasts.

"What the fuck are you doing here?" Alek kicked Yusef, prompting him to roll over.

Yusef turned onto his back and scowled at him. "I'm not telling you anything."

Alek lowered his gun and shot Yusef's other arm. "Talk."

Yusef growled, then cursed at him again until Alek aimed his gun at his dick.

"I'll keep you alive as long as I need to. Now fucking talk."

I licked my lips, scared but not terrified by the violence. I was raised with this kind of a lifestyle. My father had never outright exposed me to this kind of killing and torture, but it always existed in the peripheral of my mind.

"He's one of my father's men."

Alek glanced at me.

"Yusef," I supplied.

"You shut the fuck up, bitch," Yusef shouted. "You're a dead woman."

Alek stepped on Yusef's crotch. "Talk. Now. Don't look at her. Just tell me what the fuck you're doing here."

"I was sent to kill her."

I blinked, stunned that the man was speaking so easily. Or maybe it was difficult. He winced and gasped in pain as Alek kept his boot on his crotch, his gun aimed at his head.

"Who ordered the hit?" Alek demanded.

"Her father."

I went still, freezing at Yusef's reply. My father? He wanted me dead? I knew he never cared for me, but to wish me *dead*? I tried to grapple with this revelation without letting any emotions cloud my mind.

"If she can't serve her purpose as a virginal bride to the head of the Valkovs, she's better off fucking dead." Yusef turned to scowl at me with pure hatred in his dark eyes.

"Sergei wanted his daughter to marry the head of the Valkov family."

"That would be Pavel," Alek argued.

Yusef hissed as Alek pushed his foot down harder. "Andrey. He wanted her to marry Andrey so she'd bear a son. Or she'd keep trying until she got a son. Then Sergei would put a hit on both of them, husband and wife." He rolled his head on the floor, sneering at me on the bed. "Her virgin pussy is all that matters. Her bearing a Valkov son would be the end and complete the coup. Power would be trans-ferred." He growled, reaching uselessly for his gun with his mangled arm. "But it looks like you've already taken her."

No, not yet. But almost. I resolutely refused to let his words sink into my brain. My father wanting a coup. His eagerness to kill me off in order to get what he wanted.

Alex didn't speak, staring down at Yusef. I couldn't look away as he remained still and pensive like that, eerily calm and not alarmed. He moved like that predator again, always in charge and sure of his motions and how he held his body in the face of danger. Yusef was no longer a danger. He couldn't grab his gun, let alone aim it. His knees were shattered, and he wouldn't be running. With the copious amount of blood leaking from his body, he was damn near dead.

"And you can't blame him for wanting it. All the glory, the power. The Valkov name was once so feared and revered," Yusef taunted. "Back when your father was alive, at least." He chuckled, but the mirth seemed forced and mean, like he wanted one last chance to hurt Alek in any way he could. "He saw to that."

"What do you know of my father?" he demanded, kicking him in the nuts. "Who saw to what?" Dropping into a low crouch, he yanked Yusef up by gripping his shirt.

"Your father," the man said, smirking with a delirious tone. "I was there."

"You were where?"

"At the... shop. When Pavel shot..."

Alek shook him. "When Pavel shot what? Who?"

Yusef breathed shallower and shallower, and his head lolled to the side. "Your father."

Alek released him as though his fingers burned. Yusef slumped down, crashing to the floor littered with glass. Still, he spoke on his deathbed, confessing, "Pavel shot your father, boy. Because he wanted it all."

A few more labored breaths left Yusef's mouth, and with a gut-wrenching sob, he exhaled one last time. Blood stained the rug as his life drained from him with a steady, pulsing push.

I'd never witnessed someone's death. I knew it happened every day in our world. Violence was a way of life for the bratva, but until this moment, I'd been sheltered. I'd never been asked to handle anything that would lead to such gore and killing. The threat was always there. Every day and night, the danger of losing lives lurked so close to each and every one of us.

Until this moment, with Yusef bleeding out on Alek's rug, I'd never witnessed it firsthand. I didn't stare at him. I didn't allow myself a chance to take in a single detail of the soldier's lifeless body. Instead, I latched my concentration on Alek as he stared at the man. As long as I looked at this protective enemy, this man who'd shielded me from being murdered, I could breathe. I could see him and know that as long as he stood between me and the rest of the world, I might have a chance to make it out of here alive.

After a long, tense span of silence, he lifted his face to me. He holstered his gun and looked me over, nodding to himself. I didn't know what that nod meant, but I replied in kind. If he was seeking me out for a visual reminder that I wasn't killed, then, yes, I'd acknowledge that.

Without a word, he got to work cleaning up the mess. I couldn't have helped if I'd wanted to. I knew not a thing about transporting a dead body and handling that much blood. I was bound to the bed, and it didn't seem like a good time to repeat my request that he untie me. I didn't want to interfere with getting rid of Yusef, and I wouldn't have been much help in physically dragging him anywhere.

Instead, I faced the ceiling and stared at it, letting the activity in the rest of the room fade to a blur in the corner of my eye.

Alek took minutes to remove Yusef from the place. I didn't know where he took him, but he had to have had practice with this. A plan was likely in place for these sorts of things. After he rolled Yusef up in the rug, which must have had plastic beneath it because no blood had leaked to the hardwood floor, he disposed of him by carrying him out the front door. Knowing Alek had left me alone for those few minutes was unnerving. I was tied up, slightly naked, and vulnerable. If anyone else had intruded, I would've been dead.

But he returned shortly, leading me to assume he'd dumped Yusef out a window in the hall or something. I didn't know, and I didn't care. All I took comfort in was that Alek was back, sweeping all the broken glass and setting the studio apartment back to as much order as was possible.

He didn't speak at all throughout the entire afternoon as he handled the mess. I almost figured he'd call one of his brothers to take care of it for him, but Alek wasn't the kind of man to give others his dirty work. He dealt with it all, quietly and efficiently.

Once he finished and showered, too, I started to slip out of the numbed shell-shocked status I'd fallen into. As he returned from the bathroom, cranking out the kinks in his neck as he approached the bed, my head filled with all the thoughts and questions I'd suppressed so far.

I didn't want to dwell on my father wishing me dead. I knew I was a pawn, but it hurt deep down to know I was *that* expendable.

"What happens now?" I asked Alek as he drank from a glass of water as he stood next to the bed. He seemed calm yet pensive, and it felt like a risk to speak up.

He stared at me as he swallowed.

"What do you mean?" He set the glass down and walked closer. As he sat on the bed, I held my breath. He seemed so calm, so sure of how this would go, that it bothered me. Being kept in the dark was the way my life was supposed to go. But after hearing that I had a hit placed on me by my own father, yeah, I was eager for him to say *something*.

"What's going to happen?" I asked.

He arched one brow. "Are you asking me to predict the fucking future?"

"With my father." I struggled to swallow past the anxiety lodged in my chest at the news of how I was to be killed off. "All of it."

"The next thing that will happen is exactly what that soldier predicted."

Huh? I furrowed my brow, not following at all. *What is he saying?*

"You'll marry and sleep with the head of the Valkov Bratva."

I gaped at him, unable to inhale. "What?" *With...Pavel?*

"And your children will represent the power of the Valkovs, not the Kastavas," he declared.

He made no sense. Why would he want to see my father's goals met? And how? I scrunched my nose, staring at him and searching his face for a clue about what he meant. "By marrying Andrey after all?"

He narrowed his eyes. "I told you. You need a strong man, Mila."

Okay, not Andrey.

"How?" I shook my head, wishing something would click. "How am I going to marry the head of your Family? Who would I marry and—"

He isn't suggesting... I tried to wrap my head around what he was scheming.

His lips remained straight in a firm line as he looked me over. Then the start of a cocky smile crossed his face. "Me."

15

ALEK

Mila blinked once. Then again. Her beautiful blue eyes remained clouded with suspicion and confusion as she gazed at me. For a moment, I worried that she'd taken too many shocks in one night. Hearing that her father wanted her dead had to hurt. If the news didn't wound her, then it should've alarmed her.

But she didn't look overwhelmed or consumed with a barrage of heavy emotions. She seemed... stuck in disbelief as she gawked at me.

"You?" she asked, lifting her brows as she shifted to get comfortable on the bed.

Not for the first time, I wondered if I could risk untying her. I wanted to. After seeing Yusef break in here and aim a gun at her, I regretted keeping her confined. At that moment, she had been vulnerable and pinned in place, an easy target for anyone with a weapon. I would have rather let her protect herself, not be stuck and exposed, but a nagging voice in the back of my mind told me to reconsider.

Mila was too stubborn, too much of a fighter for me to *know* that she wouldn't try to run.

Yusef—or any other enemy—shouldn't have been able to get up here at all. When I disposed of his body in the dumpster, I took faith in the fact that he'd ruined the fire escape leading toward my floor. Unless someone rappelled down to my window from the rooftop, which was highly inaccessible with its severe slope, no one else would be coming here.

I'd almost wondered when it could happen. I'd been careful not to be tailed, but shit happened. Cameras were everywhere. People talked. The door was reinforced against being busted in, but that window was the only weak spot.

Not anymore. I frowned at Mila as she lay on the bed, stupefied by my plans.

"Me, Mila. You'll marry me."

She huffed a snarky laugh and rolled her eyes. "Yeah, right."

"Are you arguing with me?"

"Oh, like my word even counts in an argument." She shook her head, sticking with this raw disbelief. "There's a couple of small issues with your grand plans."

"Like what?"

"You're not the head of your Family. Two others stand in your way."

They won't for very long.

Realization dawned on her expressive face, and she dropped her jaw again. I was becoming fond of this phenomenon. Shocking her was rewarding, because it was proof that she was sharp and quick-witted enough to form her own opinions and stand by them. This was no idiotic woman. She was intelligent.

More than that, though, it was all too easy to picture my dick slipping into that wide-open O of her plump lips. She'd wrap them around me and take me deep. I could just tell.

"You're… going to take over your Family? You're going to oust your uncle and cousin for power?" She spoke it carefully, like she didn't trust saying those mighty and damning words aloud.

I nodded. "It's the perfect time."

She narrowed her eyes. "How so?"

"You heard what that man said." I tipped my head toward the center of the room, indicating where Yusef had died. "He was there when my father died. He witnessed it."

She struggled to sit up but couldn't. Shaking her head, she fought to protest. "No. Alek. How can you… No. You can't just take his word for that."

I tapped my fist to my chest, right over where my heart lay. "I can. Because I already knew that to be the truth. Deep down, I think I've always known. Each time I looked at my fucking uncle, I suspected that he was behind my father's death. I know it."

"You're sure?"

"My brothers will agree. We've always questioned how he'd been shot at the shop during a supposed turf war. I always wondered if he'd been set up, and I knew it had to be Pavel who'd arranged it. Because he wanted the power."

As I sat there staring at her, memories trickled through my mind. When I was younger, when my father did all the heavy lifting and work for Pavel, there were too many episodes of disagreements. Of Pavel not liking my father's influence. Of my father worrying that his brother didn't know how to handle his position as Pakhan. It was no simple overnight incidence of loathing. Pavel had always despised my father—all the way until he'd eliminated him.

"I will avenge my father. And in doing so, I will fix my Family. We have suffered too long under the wrong leadership."

She licked her lips, rapt in listening to my firm declarations.

"I'll remove Pavel. And my cousin. And with you," I said as I shifted more toward her, "I will see to a stronger generation in the future, one that will secure our influence and power that your father wants for himself."

Yusef's words had cut deep when he taunted about how my family's name used to represent such prestige and invoke such fear. Under Pavel's rule, we disintegrated into a laughingstock, sloppy and weak. As soon as I changed things up with this war, I would set us on the right path for success again.

She reacted, shaking her head slightly. "No. Alek, that can't be the right solution to this."

Are you afraid? I doubted it, and her protest amused me instead.

"This cannot be the right decision. There's got to be another way."

"This is the only solution," I countered.

"But..." She furrowed her brow. "Why *me?*"

"Because you are his daughter. He tried to send you to us as a pawn, and I will show the world what happens when anyone attempts such a grave mistake like that."

A long sigh left her lips. "But you can't actually want to... You don't want to use me like this."

"I do." *Starting now.* Having a soldier break in here was a hell of a way to ruin the mood. When Yusef interrupted, I'd been two seconds away from claiming Mila's virginity.

Now that he was gone and I had a solid plan for the future with this sexy woman, nothing could hold me back.

"But it's... I'm not—"

I shifted over to cover her, but after I kissed her quiet, I kneeled back and looked my fill.

My virgin. My woman. She was both if I had anything to say about it.

"I do want you." I shoved the towel off her breasts, letting it fall to the floor. Her eyes glittered with raw lust as I gripped the hem of her dress. The white fabric strained with her heaving chest, and with one hard yank down, I ripped the gown's bodice into two.

"Alek!"

"I can't wait to feel your pussy around my dick."

"But—"

I grabbed handfuls of her skirts next, continuing with the destruction of the damaged and bloody gown. With each tear and rip hissing through the air, I freed her of the layered mess of too much cloth. As I continued, freeing her until she lay there naked and trembling under my gaze, she wriggled and shifted.

"I'm not—"

I kissed her again, silencing her concerns. Covering her nude body was a temptation that drove me crazy. I was still dressed, but the contrast provided an extra thrill.

She moaned into my mouth but shook her head and parted her lips on a ragged draw of air. "Alek, this isn't right."

I leaned back, prepared to prove her wrong again. She could tell me *no* all she wanted, but I knew it was a lie. She wanted me. Regardless of the tumultuous news she'd heard since I almost took her, and despite the harsh violence and shock of Yusef's intrusion, she would want me again.

Picking up her legs, I took my time in staring at her bare beauty. All that creamy skin, unblemished and smooth over her sexy curves. Her breasts swayed with every motion as I draped her thighs over my shoulders. I lifted her, both hands on her juicy ass, and brought her glistening pussy toward my face as I lowered to rest on the bed with her.

One taste wasn't enough. I was fucking positive that one time fucking her wouldn't, either. She'd understand. She'd realize how badly I wanted to make my version of the future come true.

Starting with her. Right now.

I tongued her slit, collecting every drop of her sweet, tangy cream as I licked and sucked. She couldn't go far with her hands still bound, and as I looked down at her tied to the headboard, my dick hardened faster. Knowing I owned her here, that I had her trapped and helpless, made a dark sliver of sin burn fiercer within me. I wasn't a gentle lover. I didn't have a kind heart. Keeping her tied up made this all the hotter, and I realized that she would agree.

Gripping her bindings to gain leverage, she thrust her pussy to my face. She'd never done this before. Only with me. But already, she was proving to be a quick learner in going for what she wanted and showing me what drove her wild. Sucking on her clit had her coming again, and as she trembled and shivered, her thighs quivering on my shoulders, I let her ride out the waves of her orgasm as I undressed.

Keeping my gun on the bed—just in case—I stripped out of my clothes. I hadn't bothered to put a shirt on after my shower, so kicking off my pants and boxers made quick work of the remaining barriers between us.

I crawled back up to her as she still raced to catch her breath. Her legs remained wide apart with me wedged between them, but she tensed and tried to cover up. She watched me nervously as I stroked my hand on my cock, too impatient. In her eyes, I saw a naughty thrill. She wanted it. She stared at my dick with so much desire, she couldn't tell me otherwise, but beneath it all, I noticed the fear.

"Alek, wait."

I didn't, lining my leaking cockhead to her wet pussy. Holding her legs apart with my side and one hand, I pushed slightly to show her that this *was* happening.

"You want this," I said as I leaned over to suck on her tits.

"I–I don't know if—"

I gripped her hips, rocking slightly to push my dick in a fraction deeper. She tensed, holding her breath, and I waited for her to calm.

She was so skittish, but she didn't need to worry. Not this time. I liked it hard and rough, but if she could just trust me…

"You're going to take my dick like a good girl, Mila."

She stared at me, her face showing how badly she wanted the pleasure I could give her while simultaneously, she was intimidated by what it would feel like. "I—"

"Right now," I vowed as I slammed into her tight, slick heat in one long, steady thrust.

She arched her back as I drove all the way in. Her breasts swayed and shook with the jerky reaction, and I didn't wait to pull out and repeat that long thrust.

Each time I slammed in, she cried out and arched her back, but before long, she acclimated to the pain, to the pleasure. She gripped the bindings keeping her hands above her head, and with lust-filled eyes, she stared right back at me and took it.

Like a fucking queen.

My fingers dug into her flesh as I gripped her hips. I didn't let go, using this hold to pull her to me and ensure I pounded into her all the way, harder and faster, until my balls smacked her ass.

Just like before, she proved to be a noisy lover, crying, sobbing, begging, and moaning. She let me hear it all, and each time she quickened with those panting, gasping sounds, I almost came right then and there.

"Come on, Mila."

I gritted my teeth at the sheer perfection of her pussy sucking me in. I fought not to come, not yet. I wanted another orgasm out of her, and I strained and tensed all my muscles as I resisted the urge to spill my cum deep inside her.

"Come, Mila. Now."

"I can't." She whined, shaking her head, so delirious this close to the peak.

I stabbed my fingers in my mouth and wet them, then dropped them to her clit and teased her hard nub. With another brutal thrust in, she clenched around my dick in an agonizingly perfect grip. I felt her pussy spasm as she cried out louder than before, and I followed her over. A few more thrusts had me growling and dropping my head back. I growled, squeezing her hip hard as she milked me. With a final jerk as I shot my cum into her womb, I released the breath I'd been holding through my orgasm.

She shivered and went limp, sated at last. Her fingers released the bindings that she'd gripped for leverage, and I pulled up before her body melted any further.

As my dick slipped free, coated in our juices and the faint smear of her virginal blood, she hissed and flinched.

"I'll be right back." I staggered off the bed, breathing hard as she lay there and shivered. Naked and taken.

All mine.

I looked her over, victorious as I noticed her sexy flush covering her face and chest.

All. Fucking. Mine.

I'd claimed her, and as I headed to the bathroom and let her come down from the high of having sex for the first time, I knew my plan had no chance of failing.

16

MILA

My pussy throbbed as the last waves of my orgasm crested through me. Each time the fluttering sensations coursed through me, I shivered and breathed deeper.

It was… nothing like what I'd expected. So good, but too fast. Left alone while he went to the bathroom, I lay there and blanked out. Staring at the ceiling was all I could do to preoccupy myself, but I was too restless to truly zone out.

My body had never felt so charged, yet relaxed. This all-consuming warmth and utter calm wasn't like anything I'd ever experienced before. Better than any time I'd pleasured myself. Even better than when he'd made me come earlier. The let-down after sex was a heady sensation, and I couldn't help but feel overwhelmed by the intensity of what had just happened. Even though I was limp, my limbs deprived of energy as I sank onto the mattress, my mind was awake and racing.

I couldn't believe he'd just…

Taken me. He hadn't waited. He hadn't *asked*. Or I supposed he had, but it was a sketchy consent that he'd taken from me, implied by my arousal. The bastard had gotten me so worked up and ready for him, slick with my cream and begging with moans and whimpers. Yes, I had wanted him to fuck me, but now that it was over…

What have I done?

I furrowed my brows as I stared at the cracked ceiling.

What have I done? Nothing. I didn't do a single damn thing. He'd taken me. He'd tied me up and kept me captive, yet I couldn't cry rape. Although I had my doubts—evidenced by my nervousness about the action—I'd welcomed him into my body. I lacked the sexual knowledge to be confident about losing my virginity after twenty-two years of protecting it, but my ignorance didn't equal a lack of consent, not really.

I hadn't done a damn thing. He'd been the one to do it all, but deep down, I couldn't hold it against him. He'd turned me on, both with his hands and mouth as well as with what he said.

He *wanted* me, and hearing him express that desire felt entirely different from what other men had instilled in me. Yes, Alek had taken me when I had no real way to reject him, but if it had been Andrey, or Geoff, or any other horny man in our world, they would've been harsh.

Alek returned, and I tried my best to shelve my thoughts. He'd pulled on sweatpants but hadn't bothered with a shirt.

"Here," he said. Just that one simple word, full of his usual dominance as he knelt on the bed and reached for my legs.

"No. Wait. What are you—"

He firmed his lips in a thin line and shot me a hard look. Impatient and frustrated, two things he often showed me, but I didn't care. He grabbed my thighs and parted my legs, not too gently. I tensed, unsure what he had in mind until he lifted his other hand. In it, he held a wet washcloth, and I held my breath as he brought it to me. With sweeping swipes, he cleaned me up. He left twice more to rinse out the rag and continue to wipe me down. I hadn't missed the tinge of red on the white terry cloth, and I frowned at the visual evidence of my virginal blood.

Mine. The blood was mine, and it would never happen again. He'd taken something no other man would ever have, and it filled me with a deep spike of indignation. Not only had he taken it as *he* pleased, but he'd done it so quickly.

I didn't speak. I kept all my thoughts and opinions locked inside as he continued to clean me up like it was the most normal thing to do in the world. He concentrated, checking that he'd removed all the sticky cum and smears of blood. And he didn't make eye contact once.

It reminded me of how I'd done this very thing for Rosamund. This… aftercare. I was the only one who helped that woman clean up after her violently brutal scenes with her husband, my father, and whichever other men wanted in on the action.

Having someone tend to me was an extraordinary experience, and I struggled to reconcile how the man so tenderly cleaning me up could be the same brute who'd kidnapped me.

He didn't stop there. After bringing the blanket around me and making sure I was comfortable and no longer exposed, he brought over a bottle of water and food. Again, he was seeing to my needs. Without my having to ask or speak up about my basic needs, he delivered.

I wouldn't let it get to my head. He wasn't *doting* on me, but with his lack of conversation, the lack of his saying anything at all or even looking at me, it felt weird.

I couldn't tell whether he was seeing to me afterward like this out of misplaced responsibility or guilt. Or… I didn't know what. Alek tending to me was the very last thing I'd counted on.

As he reclaimed his spot on the bed, sitting next to me but not touching me, he didn't give the impression of caring. He avoided contact, it seemed, but it didn't feel like a cold detachment.

I was… his. I could sense that change. Even if he hadn't proclaimed his intentions to take me before he did the deed, his nearness spoke of a possessive nature.

I was claimed. No longer clean as a bride. My one value, my main asset, was stolen and tossed away by this man, and I fought the urge to lash out at him.

"Now what?"

He turned to face me, his brows raised at my outburst. The apartment had been so quiet and still for so long, my loud voice was jarring.

"Now what?" I repeated as the burn of tears threatened in my eyes. Did he think ahead to that? Had he considered what he'd really just done here? I was no longer a virgin. I no longer had *any* value or worth. None at all. I was used up.

All my life, I'd known my purpose. To serve the bratva men. I was a pawn. A usable, disposable *thing*, not a person, and now that he'd ripped my worth from me, I felt empty and useless. Discarded.

"I told you," he repeated as he lowered to lie next to me, facing me but not touching.

I wrestled with my bindings, and I damned them all over again. Shame crested through me at the memory of how I'd used them to push against him so I could feel the full, deep hit of his dick inside me, but now, as I struggled to acclimate to the fact that I was no longer a virgin, I loathed the constraints all over again.

"I'm… I'm *nothing* now. Just used up and—"

"Hey." He set one hand on my stomach, pushing down as I writhed and fought to get free. "Calm down."

131

"No!" I glowered at him, hating that he saw the tears leaking from my eyes. "I will *not* calm down."

"It's better this way."

"Better?" I sassed. "*Better?* I'm good for absolutely nothing now."

He shook his head, calm but irked with my outburst. "It's better this way."

"What?" I snapped, wishing I could punch his smug face. "*What* is better this way?"

His eyes turned flinty with annoyance, but I didn't give a shit. I had every right to react however I saw fit.

"You'd better watch your mouth."

"Don't tell me—"

He reached over and gripped my jaw. "If I hadn't shown up at the church and stopped the wedding, you would've been *his* wife by now."

I stilled, letting his words sink through the chaos in my mind. With clarity, I understood his point, and the ramifications of what he'd prevented chilled me. Instead of losing my virginity to Alek, I would have done so with my husband. Andrey.

Alek was a hard man, but I saw now that he could be soft inside too. He hadn't dismissed me and left me bloody, cold, and thirsty on the bed after he took me. He'd come back and tried to make me as comfortable as possible.

"You realize that?"

I sniffled, not wanting to give in and nod.

"He would've been the one to fuck you, not me. Right?"

I looked down, but he tipped my face up so I would have to maintain eye contact.

"He would have abused you. Passed you around like a fucking trophy to share."

My blood turned to ice. *Just like Rosamund's fate.* The idea of being given to multiple strangers in a gang bang... *God, no.* I couldn't help how quickly I shuddered, repulsed by the possibility of such a horror.

"You knew this. You knew going into that wedding that he would have taken you however he saw fit."

I frowned at him, wishing I could retort that he'd done the same thing. As the thought rushed through my mind, I refused to believe it. Alek *had* been rough, but he hadn't been cruel. I couldn't hold that against him, and in a sick, stupid way, I knew that this man was the lesser of two evils of what I could have accepted as my fate.

"Don't try to tell me you're outraged. You said it yourself. You've always understood your purpose. To serve your bratva men. To be in an arranged marriage."

"I know. But—"

"But nothing." He released my jaw with a firm jerk, almost angry with my attitude.

As he lay back on the bed, no longer facing me, he stared at the ceiling. "You ask what's next, but I can't understand how you can act so clueless."

"Clueless?"

"Yes, clueless. What the fuck do you think will happen?" He rolled his head on the pillow to smirk at me. "I'm not taking you back to your father. He wants you dead, remember? He's put a fucking hit on your head."

The stark reminder cut at my heart. It was such an ugly, dark truth to hear, no better news this time than it was when Yusef revealed it.

"If you'd married Andrey, he would have fucked you up. Abused you. Mutilated you."

I swallowed hard, knowing he wasn't talking out of his ass. I'd heard the horror stories.

"He would have shared you and discarded you like a fuck toy."

But you haven't. No one else was here to share me with, but I doubted it would have entered Alek's mind. He looked at me with such a possessive intensity. He'd covered my breasts when Yusef burst in. I didn't get the impression that Alek shared, not his women, not anything.

At the same time, I was too guarded to assume his actions and attitude could mean that he cared. I wouldn't let him dupe me into thinking he held me in some kind of high esteem to *care* about me that much.

"As far as I'm concerned, you're mine now, Mila."

I scoffed, shaking my head. "Yeah, as your whore." A used-up virgin. It stung to know I would still be a *thing*.

"No." He didn't face me as he argued. "No. I'll marry you."

He'd tossed out that ridiculous claim before he fucked me, and in the heat of the moment, I'd been quick to dismiss it as him talking big.

I watched him look at me, dead in the eyes. "I'm going to marry you, Mila."

Shock rippled through me as the realization dawned. He actually meant it. He intended to make me his bride, his wife.

He truly planned to make me his wife. From the altar of my arrangement to be connected with another man to this dingy apartment where I remained tied up, my marital status had changed drastically.

Marry Alek? I stared at him, waiting for him to admit it was crazy talk.

He didn't. He gazed right back at me, cool, calm, and confident about his plan.

I shared no such smug confidence. All I could think about was how he intended to involve me in this war among men.

He planned to drag me all the way through it right by his side.

17

ALEK

Now that I'd had Mila once, I wanted her again. Lying here on the bed was torture. She was within reach, just over here, an arm's length away.

I didn't move any closer. Distance would help her adjust to what I explained. I saw how much she struggled to understand, and I couldn't fault her for her naiveté. She was so damn young, so inexperienced with this world. Her father had sheltered her all her life, and now that she'd broken out of that existence, I bet she felt like her whole purpose was shattered.

I'd turned her life upside down, but I stood by my reasoning. It would be for the better. This was the only solution that would ensure my success and her survival.

Because in just these few short days that I'd known her, I didn't want to entertain the possibility of losing her. It didn't make sense how quickly and deeply she'd gotten under my skin. But she had.

I didn't plan to stop that wedding so I could take her for myself. I'd only gone to Plan B and kidnapped her so she wouldn't be able to marry Andrey. Not because I'd coveted her for myself. Now that I'd had her, now that I'd realized how fucking perfect she felt with me, I couldn't imagine releasing her.

I wouldn't be returning her to her father. I wouldn't consider letting Andrey have her now.

She was mine, and I intended to keep her.

As she lay there still and silent, brooding about what I said, I felt at ease. She could take her time. No matter how she chose to view these circumstances and no matter how she tweaked her perspective on the changes that had been forced on her, I would not change my mind.

Before her wedding, she'd been on my mind. I'd struggled to stop thinking about her, and that was from just a mere interaction at that shipping office.

Now that she'd been here with me, arguing or grinding back against me to come faster, I knew I'd never be able to cast her out of my mind.

Mila had spirit. She had fire. And she would be an ideal woman to help me bring the Valkov Bratva back to the top. I wasn't tricking myself into thinking I knew everything about her, but of the little I'd witnessed so far, I just knew. She was the kind of no-nonsense woman with the right amount of backbone to not only survive in our world, but also to contribute to it. I suspected that she was a maternal sort, a woman who would want to nurture and help. Someone who'd be inclined to help repair the chaos within my family. Women were submissive to the bratva men, but I also knew that with the right wife at my side, she could help me make the Valkov Bratva seem like a *family* again, not just an operation held together with shitty leadership.

They way things used to be, like when I was a boy and my grandfather was the Pakhan. When I was too small to understand all the violence as my grandmother helped to nurture me.

Mila staying with me—in marriage and life—had to be the solution to this mess. If I sent her home, she'd be as good as dead. Yusef couldn't have been lying when he predicted that Sergei would ensure Mila's death. I couldn't bear to think of her being taken from me like that. One time with her was nowhere near enough, and already, I looked forward to enjoying her sweet, sexy body again. Over and over, I would take my fill of her.

I glanced at her, wondering if that was the point that stuck the worst. She had to understand that she no longer had a family, no longer had a home with her father. He wanted to end her.

Pavel had never tried to kill me. We'd both viewed each other with malice and disrespect, but he'd never escalated to the point of eliminating me like a pest he didn't want to deal with any longer.

Perhaps killing me wouldn't have even mattered. Or he was too spiteful to ever lift his hand and kill the son of his brother, another he *had* murdered.

After my action at the wedding, though, I'd guaranteed a hit on my own head. Pavel was out for my blood. According to my brothers, he was furious and raging to bring me down. If he were to get ahold of me, he'd kill me on the spot. But that was different. I'd warranted that. I'd caused his fury by going against his will.

Mila had done nothing to deserve her father's wrath. She'd only served and worked as expected, going so far in her duty as to show up for that ill-fated wedding. She clung to the assumption that her virgin pussy was all that lent her any worth, but now that I had it, now that I'd claimed her, that power belonged to me.

She belonged to me.

Finally, she broke the silence with a grunt of a laugh. "You're crazy."

That's not the first time I've been called that. I bit back a wicked grin.

"We can't get married, Alek." She rolled her head on the pillow and gave me a droll look.

"We will."

She shook her hands, still bound over her head. The emphasis of her restraints amused me. They weren't cutting off her circulation. She was as comfortable as possible, but I knew I couldn't rely on them for good.

"How the hell could we get married if I'm hidden and tied up like an animal in a cage?"

Like an animal in a cage? I rolled my eyes at her theatrics. "I'll get a priest."

"To come here?" She scoffed.

"No." Ever since Yusef broke in, I debated with the urgency to relocate. If he found us here, someone else could get close. Staying stationary would be foolhardy.

"I'll make it legal. With a priest somewhere else." I held her gaze as I swore it. "You'll be my wife in every way, Mila."

Once more, she scoffed, stuck in that stubborn disbelief. "I still say you're crazy. You kidnap me from my wedding so you can plan your own with me?"

I studied her expressive face, grateful that she wasn't prone to hysterics. I doubted many other women could have this degree of levelheadedness to so calmly discuss our situation. The more I considered it, I realized this was likely the most input she'd had yet about her wedding at all. I was under no illusion that this all had to be fucking with her head. She was a captive here, under my rule as I called the shots. Still, she didn't adopt a hopelessness as my prisoner. She could... work with me.

"I didn't take you from your wedding knowing that you would instead end up being my bride."

She rolled her eyes.

"But now that the circumstances have fallen into place like this, it makes the most sense to marry."

"According to you," she sassed.

I nodded. "Yes." Of course, this would happen as I saw fit.

"I still say you're only asking for trouble to marry me."

I almost smiled, reminded of how she'd said that before. She'd told me that she knew I was trouble the first time she saw me, and I felt the same about her. The longer I spent with her, the more I came to realize that she offered a good sort of challenge in my life. Not a threat or danger.

"I agree. I'm stirring things up and welcoming chaos by marrying you. But it needs to be done. This war has to happen to change what has been the status quo for too long."

She sighed and shook her head as she nestled it on the pillow. "You're still crazy," she repeated, resigned with something like amusement in her tone. "You want to marry me, to align yourself with me as you see fit, but you don't trust me enough to untie me?"

I looked at her wound, then her bindings. "Not yet."

She shot me a beady-eyed glare as I sat up quickly and retrieved my phone from the table. I did my best to ignore the burn of her stare on me as I paced, needing to move as I set preparations in place.

First, I would contact my brothers and request their help in making my wedding possible.

If Yusef hadn't broken in here to try to kill Mila, I wasn't sure if I would've jumped as quickly on this decision to marry her. I was being rash. The idea had come to me suddenly as I disposed of the soldier's body, but I didn't require more time to think it through. Marrying her was the best logical reaction to the news of the hit placed on her by her father. And I'd stand by my choice.

I began with Nik, counting on him to show the least amount of shock with my update. He didn't pick up, though. In the time that it took me to scroll through my contacts to reach Ivan instead, Nik texted.

Nikolai: *Busy at the moment. Do you need something?*

Aleksei: *Prepare to be a witness at my wedding.*

I dialed Ivan before replying to the many texts that Nik fired my way in response.

Ivan didn't answer either, but I wasn't worried. They had to hide. They had to investigate that bullshit at the docks. Pavel had placed targets on them, and I knew they would take extreme care and caution to be safe as they did as I'd instructed.

I finally reached Maxim, and to his credit, he didn't sound distressed when he picked up.

"I need you to find a priest to officiate my marriage to Mila."

"Mila?" He coughed in surprise. "*You're* going to marry her?"

"It's a long story to explain. I will fill you in later with all the details. Right now, it's imperative that we marry as quickly as possible." I glanced at her resting. It seemed all the ups and downs had finally caught up to her and exhausted her.

"As legally as possible, too," I added. "Find a priest. Pay him to come to a secure location. Once you have it arranged, I need you and another brother to witness the ceremony."

"Fuck, Alek." He scoffed on the other line, and I bet he was raking his hand through his thick hair, his tell for being agitated. "This is... this is insane."

I smirked. "Crazy? Yeah, it is, but I know what I'm doing."

"What's the point of marrying her? I thought you were convinced that aligning with the Kastavas will ruin us."

"Not unless I take her as my bride and end their Family in the same blow."

"How?"

I paced, rubbing the back of my neck as all the stress and fighting caught up to me in a physical sense. I was tired, too, and a good night of rest would make me clearheaded enough to take Mila as my bride tomorrow.

"Because they want to use her to begin the next generation. As Kastavas, not Valkovs. She's mine now, and *I* will determine the future of her—our—children. Not Sergei fucking Kastava."

Maxim swore, immediately uneasy, as I expected he'd be. "How do you know of his plans? We're trying to get an angle on the shipment and figure out who this third party is with the Colver dock arrangement, and you seem to be going on a different approach with all of this."

"I'll explain later. A soldier snuck in to try to kill her."

"Who put a hit on her?" he demanded.

"Sergei Kastava."

As he reacted, cursing and asking more questions that I tried to answer the best I could, my patience wore thin. "You'll help me?"

"Yeah. Yes, Alek. I'll help. I'll get it ready and text you once I find a secure place," he replied.

"Good. Thank you, Brother."

After I hung up, I felt elated and excited. Stealing Mila from her wedding had caused a lot of commotion.

But I joined her on the bed knowing that marrying her in the morning would incite much more chaos.

Everything we needed to prove to Sergei, Pavel, and the rest of the world that I would be in charge from here on out.

18

MILA

For the second time in such a short span, I woke up knowing I would be married today. It would stick. I was sure that *this* wedding would actually happen.

I lay in the bed, blinking away the last traces of sleep, and knew that in a few hours, I would no longer be just myself. I would be expected to undergo another identity crisis and change who I was.

Yesterday, Alek took my virginity. That was already a huge shift to get used to. The one thing that had always defined me and kept me safe and untouchable no longer mattered.

Once I shared vows with him, though, I would no longer be Mila Kastava, Sergei Kastava's daughter. I would be Mila *Valkov*, Aleksei Valkov's wife.

The title sounded so powerful, so ultimate and unchangeable, and it would be. Women married for life in the bratva. Divorce was never an option, and spouses remained linked in name and purpose until death.

And mine will reach me swiftly if I don't do this.

If I were to run away or return to my father, I would be dead. Just because I'd been thwarted from marrying Andrey, I no longer served a usable purpose to him.

A deep sigh left my lips, but it didn't wake my intended. Alek slept away, not touching me on the bed. His gun remained in his hand, and I grew curious whether something had spooked him to want to hold it. It hadn't been there last night.

Even if someone had crept too close to our hideout here, I knew he'd keep me safe. I was now his object to treasure and use for leverage. While it stung to always know I mattered as a *thing*, not a person, I felt safer with him than I had with anyone else.

I couldn't shake off this sense of bewilderment, though. Me, marrying Alek. It seemed so surreal, but at the same time, so right. Since he'd consummated the union *before* any plans to marry me, he'd already made it as legitimate as possible. He'd already done that part, and I'd be a liar if I said I hadn't wanted it.

In a sense, I desired what he suggested because it was something I could do for myself. Power was never granted to me, and giving in to the lust for him felt like something under my control. Still, it boggled my mind as I looked him up and down, excited to have the freedom to just study him without having to explain my interest.

It baffled me how I'd gotten to this position, this moment. I'd gone from being in an arranged marriage to being in a stolen one. And still tied up within the bratva. I had been raised to know this would be my life, but I never could have counted on these twists.

The day before my wedding with Andrey, my stomach had been tense with nerves and churning on acid with no food to fill it. That potent anxiety had gripped me in an ugly sense of "jitters", but it was nothing like the nervousness that filled me now.

As I watched Alek sleep, I couldn't help but feel apprehensive about my future. I would live. I would survive. Because of him. He was promising that my father wouldn't kill me. At the same time, I felt uneasy about how I would manage being a wife. His wife. He'd already shown me a sample of how good it could be with his big, hard dick stretching me with that delicious burn of pain. I'd felt so full, but so good as he pushed me to come again and again.

That was the trickiest element about it all. Alek's... power. This man messed with my head in a way no one else had tried to, and I felt unsteady with him. He made me want him. I undeniably did. But I knew I shouldn't.

For fuck's sake, he *still* kept me tied. I didn't anticipate winning his trust, not in anything too important, but he couldn't expect to keep me trapped and bound forever, could he?

Of course, he won't. Until we left here to get married, I was a kidnapped woman. I was a bride stolen from the church. With that qualifier, these strips of fabric made sense on my hands. He wanted to get me out of marrying Andrey, and he had.

Even though it wasn't due or warranted, I did have faith that he would release me before we went. I hadn't argued against his idea to marry. I didn't tell him no, despite how I should have. He'd hear no protests from my lips, and the quicker I convinced myself, my mind, that this was my best option forward, the easier it would be to adjust to connecting my life with his.

I could do my part. *Right?* I'd never given myself a sincere hope that I could marry for love. Getting hitched with Alek was just an obligation to see through, and I would damn well make the best of it that I could. Sticking with him was preferred to returning to my murderous father since he only saw me as an expendable object to toss away.

"Second thoughts?"

I jolted at Alek's deep voice. It was so low and husky, full of sleep, and my traitorous body reacted to his smoldering gaze as I looked at his face. He'd been so still that I thought he was still sleeping. Now, I wondered how long he'd been watching me muse about my predicament.

If I admitted my nerves, it wouldn't change anything. I wanted to stand by my decision to make the best of this. I could do this. I would see this through, dammit. "No. No second thoughts."

"Hmm." He sat up, stretching and looking at his phone.

I'd fallen asleep to him talking to one of his brothers, and I realized that hearing his voice was so comforting that it could always have that effect on me. A deep, sonorous tone, lulling me to relax. I hadn't lowered my guard this much before, and I worried that he could hold such power over me.

"Maxim texted me last night that everything is arranged."

I tracked him through the apartment as he changed into the suit he'd arrived here in. "Everything meaning...?"

"He's found a priest and secured another secret location for us." He held my gaze as he pulled his shirt on, hiding his chiseled, sexy body.

"What about a dress?" I sassed back, almost laughing. The jerk ripped my bodice. My panties had been shredded in half. And my skirts were... I craned my neck, looking around the bed the best I could with this angle. I had no clue where the remains of my gown were.

"These will sort of work." Alek held up the many layers of my gown. A few rough tugs ripped the tulle and lacy filler. All that remained was a simplified shift. "And I'll find a shirt."

I huffed, amused that I'd marry without any lingerie.

"And what about these?" I wiggled my hands, bringing his attention back to my hands that were still bound to the headboard. "I can't see how you plan to drag me across town cuffed like this. Not unless you want to attract attention."

He strode to the bed, glaring at me with an undercurrent of a warning in his eyes. After he extracted a blade from his pocket, he cut through the strips of white fabric that he'd used to leash me to the bed.

My arms fell, and the material of my bindings slithered lower. Before I could move them and flex my sore muscles from the position, Alek took hold of me and ran his hot, callused hands over my flesh. With a kneading rub, he massaged my arms and lowered them. In the same motion, he guided me to sit up and swing my legs off the bed.

I moaned at his touch, relieved to have my arms back down. Blood circulated so fast that it almost dizzied me, and as he helped me stand, I shivered through the pinpricks of tingles along my skin.

He held one hand as he unwrapped the bindings from the other, then he switched to loosen the other ties. Both of his hands remained on my wrists, rubbing and caressing where the material had dug into my skin a fair bit.

"You keep moaning like that…" he threatened darkly.

"It feels so good."

"I could make you feel better," he teased, dipping low to pick me up. He collected me in his arms so suddenly, I screeched in shock. I'd been lying down so long, only up to go to the bathroom a few times, that I felt like I was topsy-turvy.

He carried me to the bathroom and set me on my feet. As he turned on the shower and then checked the gauze he'd tied on my arm, I held back a laugh. "Yeah, you can make me feel better by promising to never tie me up like that again."

His lips smashed over mine, claiming my mouth in a hard, fast kiss. I rocked back, surprised at his kiss, but he caught me with his arm around my waist.

"No," he replied, turning me to face the shower. He kept his arms around me, one hand cupping my breast as he thumbed my nipple into a stiff peak. His other hand slid lower, over my stomach, until he rubbed his palm against my mound.

I breathed in the steam from the shower. From zero to sixty, he revved me up to instant, total desire. Leaning my head back on his chest, I sighed and spread my legs wider apart, already getting used to how badly I'd want to give him the easiest access to where I ached for him.

"I can make you feel better. Like this." He stabbed his finger past my folds and collected my cream. Already, I was dripping for him. When he rocked his hips against my ass, grinding his hard-on along my crack, I breathed faster yet.

"I… Okay." I shivered under his touch, pushing back against his cock trapped in his pants. He kissed along my neck, sucking hard and leaving his mark, and fingered me so expertly, I was soon riding his hand the best I could. I needed his guidance. I wanted his help, but he had other ideas yet.

"And if you behave, I'll always make sure you feel good." He unzipped his pants and let his dick spring out. As the long steely length of his erection prodded at my ass, he dipped at his knees to rub it along my crack.

"Oh, fuck." I whimpered, letting out raw sounds that made no sense as he resumed fingering me. He wasn't penetrating me. Only his digits pistoned into my slick heat. But the taunting pressure of his hardness thrilled me. I wanted it. I wanted him, but most of all, I wanted to be his good girl and be rewarded with his thick dick filling me again.

"Yeah, *oh, fuck*," he mocked as he pushed me forward.

I stumbled just a bit as I stepped into the shower. Water crashed over my head, plastering my hair to my face as I braced my hand to the tiled wall of the stall. I huffed and squinted through the water. He didn't leave, standing there with his tempting dick standing to attention.

"I'm getting tired of that."

He grinned, staring at me in the water as he fisted himself and lazily stroked. "Tired of what?"

"Your just… stopping." I rubbed my thighs together, needing some kind of friction to relieve myself of the tension of being so close to coming.

"Withholding your orgasm?" His grin widened.

I lowered my gaze to his cock, mesmerized with his steady tug on it.

"If you want it," he drawled, "if you want me to make your pussy feel good…" He growled and stroked himself faster.

Seeing him jerk off like this fucked with my logic. All I could do was stare and get more turned on. I breathed faster, slipping my hand toward my sex to play right along with him. The second I touched my clit, he released himself and slapped my hand away.

"No. *I* get to decide when you come."

I gawked at him, so hot and bothered and furious that he'd tease me. He couldn't just leave me hanging like this!

He grabbed a folded washcloth from a shelf, still not bothering to tuck his dick back into his pants. "And if you want to come, if you want my dick, you won't think about running."

I opened and closed my mouth. Words failed to come. I was stuck, torn between wanting to jump at him and touch his dick bobbing around and teasing me so openly and telling him off. I wasn't something to just tease and torment. It wasn't fair.

Instead, I clamped my lips shut and ripped the washcloth out of his hand.

"You hear me?" he asked, still too smug and proud about how he had me right where he wanted me.

I glowered, refusing to give him the satisfaction of an agreement.

He had me there. I hated that my body was so quick to betray me, but my lust didn't lie.

I wanted him, all right, and against my better judgment, I wanted his dick again, dammit.

As I cleaned up, I growled to myself and tried not to think ahead to how much better it might feel when he filled me again.

Because when that time came, he'd own me.

I'd be his wife. To fuck and fill—however he liked.

But I'll be damned if he makes me admit how much I want it.

19

ALEK

Teasing Mila in the bathroom caused more harm than good. I had her right where I wanted her, but I'd also made myself distracted with lust.

She wasn't going to run. I couldn't know that with one hundred percent confidence, but she wasn't stupid. She'd heard Yusef. She realized the real and waiting risks that she would face if she decided to bolt from me. I'd proven to her that she would be better off *with* me. I'd protected her under gunfire. I'd pleasured her like no one else ever had. I didn't want to assume that she would think she owed it to me to stay and not run. But I hadn't hesitated to manipulate her, to taunt her into being so close to an orgasm, only to stop her before she could find her release.

Stupid. It was a huge mistake on my part because I'd gotten turned on too. Shoving my cock along her ass had tempted me too far, and as I rubbed my erection, letting her watch me and see what she did to me, I pushed myself too far.

We'd left the studio apartment and headed toward the location Maxim had secured for our impromptu wedding. And with every step

I took to close the distance to that address, I fought the lingering threads of potent desire.

She wore the mismatched outfit that I'd cobbled together, and walking alongside me, she couldn't have been more gorgeous. A plain brown sack would have done her justice. She had that classic, bone-deep kind of graceful beauty, such that she would be appealing no matter what she wore.

Especially when she wears nothing. I gritted my teeth at the vision of her in the shower, naked and tempting with all that water streaming over her smooth skin.

She was messing with my mind, and as I tried to ignore the burning ache of desire, I worried that I would be too distracted to keep her safe on the streets. Already, I'd glanced at her more than a handful of times. Her hand remained tight in mine, but my focus was skewed. Anyone could try to get a jump on us out here. I didn't need to be looking at her. I had to maintain a careful diligence and scope our surroundings, to be alert and keep a lookout.

Soon enough, we encountered trouble on the way. I was armed. I was ready to fight, but with Mila with me and no backup that I could see, I didn't want to risk her being hurt at all.

"Look." A thug from the Ortez Cartel elbowed his buddy, and a group of five of them turned toward us as we moved to walk by.

"A Valkov?" another taunted. "You a lil' lost, man?"

Two approached with a glint of metal reflecting light. They'd flicked their knives open upon seeing me, and I stepped in front of Mila as they tried to surround us.

She stayed behind me, close, until it would've been dangerous to stay near my arms as I fought back. They were green, too new to this life of crime, and I easily fought them back. Three ran, and two remained unconscious on the ground.

"You all right?" I asked Mila once I settled that interruption. My protective instincts kicked into high gear, but seeing her close by and not looking that rattled, I calmed down faster.

She accepted my hand and commenced walking down the sidewalk with me. We headed out of there faster, and she glanced back over her shoulder just the once. "Yeah. I'm fine."

And she was. I saw that she was. She hadn't fainted or cowered. No screams left her mouth and attracted more trouble. This was twice that she'd been subjected to violence firsthand, and she hadn't freaked out. Then again, I recalled that she hadn't acted like a baby or wimped out when I fucked her roughly. She wasn't so sheltered that she couldn't stomach some ugliness from life.

Maybe she is the perfect woman for me, after all. Dealing with a more delicate woman who couldn't handle the high stakes of our world would be a headache.

First and foremost, marrying her was a necessary power play. She was part of my strategy now. I would undermine Sergei's attempt to con my bratva. And I would begin the process of overthrowing Pavel and Andrey by taking her for myself.

At the same time, it didn't hurt to consider a mutually beneficial union. It seemed too foolhardy to wish for a happy life full of love with this woman, but something like a simpler compromise of part- nership wouldn't hurt anything. She'd more than proven how stalwart and unshakable she could be in the most stressful moments.

Without any further interruptions or incidents, we arrived at the location Maxim had directed me to. It wasn't a warehouse, but a mostly abandoned office building. Offices stood empty and bare, showing signs of neglect and disrepair. The tall structure was likely on a list of condemned buildings to be torn down, and it was perfect for a clandestine meetup with a priest for a hasty wedding. No one would be in here to stop us.

But the moment we entered the room I was instructed to find, I knew how wrong I was to hope and assume that we would have security and privacy here.

We opened the door and walked into a scene of chaos and gore.

Mila gasped. Her hand flew to cover her mouth, and her eyes opened wide with shock. I gripped her hand tighter as I held up my gun again.

Only one perpetrator stood in here, determined to stand in my way.

The priest lay slumped on the bare hardwood floor. Blood puddled around his chest as his body jerked with wheezy, labored breaths. The bald man was one inch from death, his eyes squinting at the ceiling as his thin lips trembled. He spoke, whispering to himself, no doubt in prayers as he dreaded his end coming near.

To the left of him, Maxim, slumped against a chair, had just taken a hit from my cousin. Blood streaked from my youngest brother's brow, and he pressed his hand to his side and hissed in pain.

He'd been beaten. I already knew he had been, but I hadn't planned on walking in here and witnessing a repeat of an attack in real time.

Another Valkov soldier remained unmoving on the other side of the room. He was likely the backup witness I'd requested my brother to find to further validate my wedding here.

In a bizarre twist of karma, Andrey had come here to stop *my* wedding. He bared his teeth at me as he turned to face us as we came into the room. As the door clicked shut after us, Mila flinched, stepping closer to me.

My fucking cousin. He was here, ready to try his best at ruining my agenda.

I tensed. All my muscles locked tight as I braced to fight him. Holding Mila's hand, I edged her to stand behind me, but she misinterpreted, damn near hiding right at my back. Her fingers curled into my suit jacket, and I loathed the slight tremor in her grip on me.

"You," Andrey spat, fuming with wild eyes as he looked between me and Mila. "Both of you." A long growl left his lips as he charged forward.

I didn't need an explanation to figure out that he must have learned about my plan. Maxim wouldn't have told him. All of my brothers knew better than to let anyone find out about what I'd tried to make happen here. But of all four of them, Maxim would be the least experienced with subterfuge. It was his only flaw, but a forgivable one at that. I couldn't count on completely slipping under the radar with war breaking out on the streets.

I had no doubt that Andrey had killed the other soldier I'd needed as a witness. He had to have wounded the priest, and Maxim too.

And that was where his wrath would end. I demanded it. His interference would stop now.

I met him head-on, fists slamming into him as he breathed ragged, hard heaves of air and tried to beat me to a pulp. In a frenzy of action, I stayed on him, determined to make him pay once and for all for getting in my way.

I'd be damned if he tried to foil me, but pure rage was driving him. Like a beast, not a man, he launched himself at me. Each time I got the upper hand with a strong hit or block, he'd double back against all odds and damn near change the tide.

One look at Mila was my downfall. I glanced at her, checking that she wasn't near the realm of danger as we fought, but that mere glimpse was all the opportunity he needed to knock me to my ass.

I skidded back, slamming my shoulder into the floor so hard that it pushed all the air out of my lungs.

By the time I slowed in the drop, grunting through the pain, he'd turned and reached for his gun. I hadn't understood why he didn't use it on me, but I realized too late that maybe he'd welcomed the fury of the fight. For the first time, he'd wanted his hands dirty—with my blood.

In slow motion, my world blurred. All my senses tripped into a smear of panic, and I felt trapped, paralyzed in place as I watched him twist and aim his gun at Mila.

She hadn't run. She stood there, creeping closer to Maxim and the priest. As soon as she spotted the real and present danger pointed her way, she went still, staring wide-eyed at Andrey snarling at her with a malicious grin.

"No." She didn't beg it weakly. It came out as a firm but too-quiet order.

"Fucking whore." He lifted his arm, and I scrambled to stand. Time stopped. My heart thundered faster with utter terror as he prepared to kill her himself.

I lurched in front of her just in time, hissing at the pain exploding in my side as I reached her.

"Alek! No!" She reached for me, her hands grabbing at my jacket as I slid right back down to the floor, landing harder than I had the first time.

20

MILA

Alek slammed against me, knocking us to the ground. My ears rang with the blast of the gun fired so close, and I sucked in a quick breath and held it. Terror held me in its grip, and I did my best to break Alek's fall.

He was too large to buffer his drop to the ground. Combined with his tackle, the force of his taking the bullet Andrey had aimed at me, and the sketchy stance I'd stood with as I tried to shrink out of my former fiancé's sight, I was on my ass. Flat on my ass, stunned by the juddering impact of being brought down.

My life had flashed before my eyes. The second Andrey pointed his gun at me, I swore I felt my essence slipping away. My soul faded and my vision blurred with extreme horror. This was it, the moment I would be done with my time in this life.

But Alek had other plans. He dove in front of me, taking the hit of the bullet, and I scrambled to keep up with the frantic change of events. My mind lagged. My senses were sluggish. I felt as though I looked through tunnel vision, vaguely able to know what was what. My reaction time was delayed, hence my rough fall, but the throbbing hit of crashing to the floor jolted me. It jarred me to wake the fuck up, to move, to be smart and help this big, strong man who'd been my hero more than he'd proven to be an enemy.

"Alek," I repeated as I panicked and felt over his body. He replied in a groan, twisting on my lap, but he couldn't get up. A warm flood of blood from his shoulder and back reached my dress, and I groped and felt around to try to stem the bleeding.

"You think you can trade up?" Andrey sneered at me. "Or down?" He laughed, brutish and loud as he watched Alek moan in agony.

"Fuck off," the other man shouted.

Maxim? I couldn't recall which of Alek's brothers was supposed to meet us here. Which one Alek had spoken with on the phone. He resembled the wounded man on my lap, though, and I knew he was trying to help.

I doubted he could do anything from that weak position against the chair. My heart hammered as I did inventory, rushing to make sense of what was most urgent. Alek was breathing harshly on my lap. He lived, for now, but with how heavy he was on me, I was trapped on the floor and unable to move him to access his wound.

Maxim wasn't much better off. Red stains littered his white shirt, and he dragged in air with rough, ragged inhales as he tried to stand with the chair's assistance.

And the priest… I checked a glance at him as well, nervous when I saw that he'd ceased mumbling his prayers to himself.

The other Valkov near the door was dead, unmoving and stiff.

That summed it up to zero. I had *no* chance for help in here, and I'd have to rely on myself.

"You want more, huh?" Andrey stalked over to Maxim and pistol whipped him for speaking up, and Alek groaned, trying to stand as he covered my hand that I'd pressed at his wound. My legs shook from the adrenaline wiring through me, but my knees ached with the pressure of keeping his large body over me. I couldn't tell whether he was too wounded and winded to get up, but I figured it would be smart to stay together. As one. If I could protect him half as much as he'd protected me, I would.

"You stupid fucking whore," Andrey taunted as he returned to me, lifting his gun again. Grinning maniacally like that, he looked deranged, insane and unstable, high on the opportunity to kill these men. His words were directed at me, but I didn't give a shit. He'd ceased mattering to me the moment Alek busted me out of that church. Andrey failed to have any meaning in my life the second Alek took my virginity.

I was no longer anything to Andrey, but it seemed like he didn't agree.

"You shouldn't have run from the Family, you stupid fucker. You shouldn't have tried to run and start a war like that," he shouted. He aimed the gun at Alek, smirking as he wiped blood and sweat from his brow. "You stupid, good-for-nothing piece of shit." His foot connected with Alek's thigh, and since he was draped over me, I felt the residual hit of Andrey's boot shoving him back with the brutal kick. I clung to him, hugging him the best I could even though it wouldn't make a difference in his fate. It wouldn't make a difference in his pain, either.

I didn't know what else to do. I wanted to stop this madness. I needed to get us out of here alive, but I was stuck, like always.

"War was overdue," Maxim argued, coughing around his words as he hung over the back of the chair. He was too weak, limited in his ability to stand, but I knew what he was doing.

Stalling. He was delaying the inevitable, pulling this madman's focus away from his brother. Alek must have realized it too, because he growled and gritted his teeth, straining to get up. Through slitted eyes, he caught my attention and leaned toward me.

Was he trying to get up? Fight back? Or was his pain too hard on that side? I couldn't understand, but after Andrey punched Maxim back to silence and stomped his way back toward us, I felt it.

Alek wasn't so cocky and confident to get up like this. He wasn't fidgeting. He'd only been trying to get his gun. I felt the hard press of it, wedged between our bodies. The barrel of the firearm pulled against my skin, and I slipped my hand to my thigh to try to grip it and pull it out. A weapon would help, but only if I could use it in time.

"Only thing that was overdue is getting rid of *you*," Andrey vowed nefariously. He lifted his gun that dripped with blood from Maxim's face. Drops plopped down through the air as Andrey pointed the end of his barrel directly at Alek's head, but I was faster.

As his trigger finger twitched, I lifted Alek's gun and aimed. I didn't hesitate. I didn't second-guess myself. I fired the gun right at Andrey's chest in the same moment that I hauled Alek closer to me. My fingers slipped on his bloody shirt, but I gained enough of a grip that I could pull him toward me.

Just in time.

Just out of the way of Andrey's bullet embedding into the floor where Alek's head had rested a second before.

Andrey groaned, slapping his hand to his wound that gushed blood. His gun fell from his hand as he pressed the through and through gunshot wound I'd given him. With a furious sneer, he stared at me as he stumbled back a step.

I kept the gun trained on him, letting him see that I had pulled the trigger. That I was the one who'd ended him. My fingers shook with a fine tremor, but I remained rigid and stubborn, not faltering in my focus on him. If he tried anything at all, I'd be ready to fire again.

It was a clean, direct hit right at his heart. His ribcage was shattered, and his vitals were plummeting. He rocked forward and sank to his knees as he lowered his chin. Still staring at me, likely damning me to hell, he slumped to the side like a ship going under.

Gravity finished his drop, and his legs kicked out as his body folded to the floor. He wheezed, breathing faster. Once blood trickled past his lips, I knew it was over.

I'd stunned us both. He probably hadn't counted on me to stand up for myself—to stand up for Alek and go to such a length to protect him.

But I had.

I killed him.

I *killed* a man. Not just anyone, but the heir to the Valkov Bratva.

My nerves were already frayed. Inside my mind, thoughts and rational connections struggled to connect and fire. In a shell-shocked state of stupor, I breathed hard and willed my heart to keep up with this suspense and danger.

The sheer incredulity, too.

I killed him.

I'd never used violence like this, not directed at anyone, but more than that, I'd never, ever been in the position to take someone's life.

Alek moaned, rolling his head to see his cousin dead on the floor. I snapped out of the haze of pure shock and ran my hands over him. My fingers were coated with blood from the wound on his shoulder, but as I hurried to check him over, I realized the bullet hadn't entered straight through him. He must have twisted as he'd tackled me, leaving his shoulder and back to take the brunt of that bullet grazing him deeply.

"Are you...?" I couldn't speak. My vocal cords were stiff, frozen from the shock, but I didn't need to talk. Alek understood my tentative and probing search over him. He nodded weakly, grimacing as I tried to lay him on the floor.

Once I had him off my lap, I could kneel and peer at him closer. He was in pain, no doubt, but he was alive and breathing. No vital organs had been impacted or severed.

"I…" I swallowed hard, my mouth so dry that I could have sworn I'd spent a week screaming to make it this hoarse. Only the adrenaline did this. It was just the shock of the events that had me jittery and mute.

Once more, I looked at Andrey's lifeless eyes staring back at us, and I tuned out the grisly sensation of the dead's attention.

Alek breathed steadier, keeping his hand over his wound. "I'm…" He nodded again, giving up on voicing the fact that he would make it.

Knowing he was stable, I crawled to my hands and knees and checked on the others. That man by the door was a lost cause, but Maxim and the priest, they were hanging in there.

I staggered to Maxim, pulling a strip of lacy ornamentation from the remains of my wedding gown's skirt. It wasn't much for a gauze or bandage, but I used it to compress the bloodiest spot on his side.

"Stabbed me," he muttered after hissing at my touch.

I nodded, checking him over quickly for any other deep injuries. I saw none that bled as much as the gash on his side, and I brought his hand toward the folded-up bunch of fabric.

"The priest." He tipped his chin toward the man, grinding his teeth as he slumped into the chair. "He was stabbed too."

I nodded, not wasting another second to hurry to the religious authority. He prayed yet, mumbling for forgiveness, and I was so edgy, so overwhelmed by the action, that I almost laughed. Forgiveness? From whom? Or *for* whom?

He didn't protest as I slipped his colorful stole free from his shoulders. I didn't know what it was called, but the long length of multicolored blue and black ceremonial material was an ideal compress for the knife slashes on his torso and up near his neck.

I supposed he was right to pray to his god. If Andrey had aimed his blade just a fraction higher, the priest wouldn't have lasted this far.

Satisfied that they all seemed stable, I scrambled back to Alek. As I rejoined him, I glanced again at Andrey.

I killed him.

I actually killed someone! Shock kept my observations detached, as though I wasn't myself but another bystander looking in. I couldn't make sense of the gravity of what I'd done.

"Mila..." Alek groaned as he tried to sit again, but I kept him down and ripped off more lacy material to stem his bleeding.

I couldn't have left them unattended. I was no nurse, but it was in my nature to help them. Just like I did for Rosamund and others in my bratva. If I had the power to show another person pity and compassion, I wouldn't hesitate.

But a careful glance around the room showed me that they would make it. All three of them. Maxim, the priest, and Alek. They'd live, and with that simple goal ensured, it was the perfect time to look out for myself.

I can run. I could get up and sprint out of here. I'd done my good deed. I'd assisted them with their wounds. None of them were in any condition to chase me down, and I knew without a shadow of hesitation that this would be my chance. This was the window of opportunity I needed to be free to run and get away at last.

But I didn't. I remained lodged right here as I glanced again at Andrey.

I'd just taken out the heir of the Valkov Family. I'd done so for the sake of saving Alek, but that detail didn't change the fact that I'd pulled the trigger and ended Pavel Valkov's son.

My intended husband—my *former* fiancé.

Alek had taken that role, and as he grabbed my hand, I squeezed his fingers back.

I'm a dead woman walking now.

I couldn't run. I had nowhere to go. Not a single place on earth would keep me safe from the reality that I'd killed Andrey Valkov.

I swallowed hard and lowered my gaze to Alek.

I don't want *to run.* With a deep, long look from him, I understood that he was asking me the silent question.

Would I stay? Or would I go?

I knew the choice I had to make. Nothing was strong enough to make me bolt and leave him like this now. I was already in too deep to do anything other than to want him, to care for him. I couldn't figure out when or how it had happened, but sometime between his visit to the S.T.L. headquarters offices and the moment I killed to protect him, I'd fallen into a trap of wanting to keep him in my life.

I shook my head, holding his hand. I wasn't going anywhere, and there was only one way to prove it.

After I strained to clear my throat, I lifted my face and addressed the priest.

"Can you still marry us?"

21

ALEK

The priest didn't answer, fumbling with sounds and stuttering like he didn't know how to reply.

She tried again, asking louder as she remained near me on the floor. "Can you still marry us? Can you stand?"

Unbelievable. It was so fucking impossible that I struggled to convince myself of what she said, of what she wanted.

She wanted to run. I knew it. I saw it in her eyes. Those beautiful blue orbs had been so hesitant, torn with the urge to flee and abandon me while I was down.

But she hadn't. She chose to stay here and still wanted to get married to me.

I glanced again at Andrey and considered why she'd be so eager to align herself with me. She'd just murdered a prominent man in a rival bratva. She'd be hunted. Targeted. Alone and without support, she'd never make it. Married to me, though, she'd have some protection.

Anyone who wanted to punish her for killing Andrey would have to go through me first. She knew it. But I suspected she wanted to stay for another reason.

As I sat up with her help, dizzy from the bullet that Andrey had aimed at her, I realized that this bold, sexy woman was made of much stronger stuff than I'd first thought. She may be young, naïve, and stubborn as fuck, but she was mature with an old soul. And she cared. I'd suspected that she was a maternal nurturer, and she'd more than proved it. She showed me how much compassion and courage she had to help me with my wound, then to see to my brother's comfort. And the priest's as well.

It should've been an oxymoron, calling her a compassionate, caring woman when she'd just murdered a man, but even in that, she'd been selfless. She'd shot him to spare my life.

"Careful," she chided as I got to my feet shakily. Her small hands braced me as she offered physical support to stand.

You care. It was a monumental concept to understand, but I felt stupid to fight against it. She'd already shown how much she cared. Despite her sass and ease with arguing with me, she gravitated toward me with affection. Like when she'd woken up in the middle of the night, still half asleep and seeking my touch and warmth on the bed. Already, she craved my touch. It gave me all the fuel to look forward to what waited ahead of us. I wanted to think that this primal desire sizzling between us could be the starting point of something that would evolve and grow into love, a deep, lasting bond with respect and need. A partnership like what my grandparents had so long ago.

"I can," the priest said as Maxim approached him and helped him to his feet. While Mila draped my arm around her shoulders and guided me toward the man Maxim had paid to be here to officiate the wedding, footsteps thundered down the hall. With Mila's support, her shoulder wedged in my armpit to stabilize me, I grabbed my gun from her hand.

My injury protested. Fierce stabs of agony lanced down my arm as I held my gun up, but I was used to being pushed to my limits.

Just as the door flew open and one of Andrey's closest confidants rushed in, I aimed my gun at his head.

He flung his hands up into the air as he skidded to a stop, breathing hard. "Aleksei?" He narrowed his eyes, looking at Mila with me, then Maxim and the priest. Last, he noticed Andrey dead next to the other Valkov soldier.

"What the fuck is going on?"

"You're going to stand right there and bear witness to our wedding." When he opened his mouth to shout back, snarling at what I'd said, I took one step closer with my gun trained on the spot between his eyes.

"This is bullshit! What the fuck are you trying to do, Aleksei?" He advanced, but Maxim lifted his gun to aim it at him as well.

He quieted, swearing and rubbing one hand over his face.

Under gunpoint, he'd behave. I glanced at the terrorized priest. "We need two witnesses?"

He gulped, his huge Adam's apple wobbling as he nodded quickly. "Yes. Two."

"Go on, then," Mila said, glancing at this newcomer who fumed at us together.

"Do you take Aleksei Valkov to be your husband, now and forever?" the priest asked her.

"I do." She glanced at me, then frowned at the man Maxim and I kept under gunpoint.

"Do you take…" The priest faltered, volleying a nervous look at Maxim, then Mila. He raised his brows, sheepish.

"Mila Kastava," she supplied, rolling her eyes. "Quickly."

"Do you take Mila Kastava to be your wife, now and forever?" he asked me.

"I do." I slammed my lips to hers without taking my eyes off the soldier near the door.

The priest dropped his jaw, blinking in shock from the fast pace of the vows. Maxim had to have warned him to keep this short and simple. As the elderly man winced in pain and pressed the cloth to his wound, I knew he'd appreciate this hasty ceremony.

"Rings?" I asked my brother.

He handed them over, and as we both kept an eye on the soldier getting angrier and angrier at the door, Mila and I slipped the simple bands onto each other's fingers. Dmitri had texted that he was still looking for our mother's ring, somewhere at the mansion my father had once shared with Pavel, but he hadn't been able to locate it yet.

Later. I'd give my wife anything she fucking wanted, all the jewels and gems in the world. Everything she coveted, I'd deliver.

"You're nothing but a fucking traitor," the soldier accused. He pointed at Andrey on the floor and twisted his lips as he struggled to keep a lid on his temper. "You've betrayed us all. You've betrayed the Family!"

I tilted my head to the side, peeved with his outburst.

"Who killed him?" he demanded.

"I did." I stood as tall as I could, ignoring the biting stabs of pain in my shoulder and back. I would never let Mila take the blame for Andrey's murder. She didn't deserve that fault. "And you're going to run home and tell him. Tell Pavel the good news."

"That you shot his son?" he shouted, reaching for his gun.

I fired one shot at his hand, hitting my mark perfectly and preventing him from trying anything else. He'd live, if with a nasty scar.

He dropped to one knee, hugging his mangled arm to his chest as he reacted.

"Go home. Tell Pavel the good news. That I've ended the waste of life that he called his son." I tightened my arm around Mila. "And that I've claimed a wife." Without looking away from him as he rocked and cradled his arm in pain, I pressed a quick kiss to her temple.

The faster he could relay this information, the quicker my uncle would be pushed to losing it. I needed him off balance, riled up, and crazy with how messily his world was crumbling apart.

"Fuck you. You'll never get away with this, Aleksei!" He staggered to his feet, weaving in his steps as he turned and rushed out the door, still holding his arm up protectively.

Once he was gone, I checked that the priest was still standing. Maxim, too. They needed medical help, and I wouldn't keep them here and prevent them from getting it.

My younger brother sighed, stepping closer with relief and worry mixed in his troubled expression. "You're all right?"

I nodded. With Mila, I sure as fuck would be. "You?"

He winced but nodded. "Before you go," he said, quick to know that we couldn't linger here. After he reached into the pocket on the inside of his jacket, he handed over papers.

"What's this?"

"Nikolai snagged them from a Kastava guard near the Colver dock." He raised his brows, wondering if he'd need to explain further.

He didn't. I flipped the papers open, spotting the familiar coded lines of gibberish. These were more copies of that same encrypted correspondence that I'd been hoping to use for answers about that big shipment. That trade was intended to damage the Family, and I hoped that these new papers would shine light on *how* Sergei Kastava planned to set the Valkovs up.

"Thank you." I refolded the packet of papers, aware of Mila watching me with an unreadable expression. Once I slipped them inside my jacket, secure in my pocket, I realized that she had yet to look away.

Her curiosity intrigued me, but it wasn't the time or place to put her on the spot about her observations and the strange way she stared at me.

For all I knew, she was just zoning out, skittish and slow to react or think after all that had happened. She'd just killed a man, and I bet it was the first time she'd taken a life. She'd just married me, and I knew she had to have mixed feelings about that after that brief moment of her hesitating to flee the scene.

I'd cut her some slack. Just a little. Once we were out of here and I saw to my wounds, I would focus on helping her adjust to our new life.

Eliminating Andrey was a huge, important step in my agenda, and I couldn't have anticipated how soon he could've been taken out of the picture. I had assumed that I would need to hunt him down and draw him out of hiding, but no. His ego, his pride, had brought him here with a lame attempt at foiling me.

"Until I see you next time," Maxim told me, leaning in for a feeble pat on the back. He didn't touch near my wound, but still, we were both running on fumes from the extent of our beatings. I knew without asking that he'd handle the bodies in my wake.

"You too, *Sister*," he added with a sly smile for Mila.

She dipped her chin in acknowledgment and shifted her weight on her feet.

Curious or not, she was mine—now and forever, like the priest had declared.

It was the fastest, bloodiest wedding I've ever witnessed, but it was over.

We were married, and it was time to get my wife out of here.

22

MILA

Alek limped with my assistance, but I worried what would happen on the sidewalks. He'd been in better health and was uninjured when those cartel members tried to stop us on our way to our wedding. Now, he was still in pain, shot and beaten, and not as fast to fight. If anyone tried to bother us on the return trip to the apartment, it would be up to me to somehow defend us.

I'd gotten lucky with that shot at his cousin. I'd killed Andrey because he was within such a close range. It was still a miracle of a shot. I knew how to operate a gun, but my aim and accuracy left much to be improved.

I didn't need to worry for long. Maxim saw us to the first floor and led us back to a garage exit. A car was waiting for us, and it was only then that I realized we might not be going back to the first place where he'd kept me.

Alek held the door open for me to enter the passenger side. After he shut the door, he rounded the car with his brother. They continued to speak in hushed tones, but their conversation was over by the time my husband opened the driver's door and got in with a deep wince of pain.

"It would be better to keep moving," he said for an explanation after he started the car and drove out of the garage.

"In here?" I asked, feeling stupid to misinterpret what he'd said. Of course, we wouldn't just stay in the car.

"We'll go to another hideout," he replied dryly, still wincing at the moment as he flexed his arm.

I'd wondered if he'd move me somewhere else after Yusef had burst in through the window, but as I thought back to all that had happened, it dawned on me that the incident had only happened yesterday. Not even a full twenty-four hours ago. Time had blurred so fast, so many things happening so quickly with a violent pace of life and death.

In the blink of an eye, I was married. Before that, I'd suddenly lost my virginity. Just as rapidly and unexpectedly, I'd killed a man.

My life was becoming a tumbled series of unfortunate and bizarre events, and all I could do was hold on and make the best of it that I could. I'd wished so desperately for another option. When my father told me that I would need to marry Andrey, then later, when he instructed that I report to him after my marriage, I'd dug deep and wished from the bottom of my heart for an alternative to my fate, that someone else from the bratva could be the bride, that a marriage could wait. Anything.

It turned out that there was something else waiting for me. Marriage. Murder.

Alek. I turned and watched him drive as he eventually pulled into another underground parking area. This garage was darker and seemed more abandoned, but with the anchored cameras on the walls and the shadows of men patrolling in the area, I knew this place was more secure. It had to be a residential property within the Valkov territory.

"Will we be protected here?"

"My men will keep us safe," he replied as he parked close to an elevator.

"*Your* men?" Already, he was assuming the position of power over his Pakhan. I'd killed Andrey for him in the spur of a moment. That was one of the two figureheads gone, but Pavel was still out there. He would be furious by now, hearing about our wedding and his son's death.

A death you *took the blame for.* I wouldn't forget how he'd protected me, taking the blame.

"Close friends and soldiers who have listened to me for the last seven years while my uncle neglected his power," he said as we walked toward the elevator. He limped slightly, but he didn't look like he needed my assistance to move inside.

Once we were in the elevator, I took in the details. Clean floors. Sleek, mirrored walls. If just this elevator looked so nice and well-maintained, I wondered what this new place would be like.

"They swear their loyalty to me." He reached out and took my hand in a rough grip as we rose to the upper floors. "My uncle will not be happy with the news."

I smirked at him. "No, really?"

He sighed. "But it had to be done."

I squinted. "Is this your way of thanking me for saving your life?"

He sobered, studying me closely as the elevator came to a stop. "Why did you?"

I swallowed hard, put on the spot to explain myself. It was simple, even though I felt vulnerable to admit it. "I didn't want you to die yet."

"*Yet?*" He led me out of the elevator car into a hallway lined with plush carpet. At the end of the corridor, he opened a door to a spacious apartment. With actual rooms and décor, this looked like a home. It was a far cry from the one-room abode where Yusef shattered all the glass and informed me of the hit placed on me.

"I didn't run," I shot back as I surveyed the large living room and took in the details of this new place.

"Why not?"

I let my shoulders droop in defeat. On one hand, I was grateful that he wasn't giving me a chance to say that I hadn't considered taking off. On the other hand, I was nervous to tell him that I *needed* him. I couldn't have run and lost his protection after I'd killed the heir to the Valkov Bratva. Because it wasn't only a matter of needing this strong, protective man. It was quickly becoming a matter of wanting him against my better judgment.

"Because I wanted to stay. With you."

He grunted in reply, pulling me through the apartment and into the bathroom. "Any good at stitches?" he asked.

I grimaced but nodded regardless. "A few times, my…" I wasn't sure what to call Rosamund. "I was expected to help with some injuries." Telling him that I had been required to do my best and stitch up Rosamund's split flesh would instill much confidence in my abilities. "I can try," I amended.

He turned, working on removing his jacket, and I got closer to help him get his garments off. Blood had the fabric sticking to his skin, and he sat on the bench in the voluminous bathroom while I wiped off the blood and sweat. Over and over, I dipped a washcloth into the sink. Red, then pink, the basin filled with his blood until it was mostly clear.

Unlike the other apartment, this one was stocked with ample first-aid supplies, and I had more than enough to work with to begin stitching him. I doubted the topical cream numbed his flesh adequately, but he didn't flinch as I did my best to sew up the gash on his shoulder and back. I was no doctor, but I was certain I was helping, not hurting, the situation.

"Is this…" I sighed, hoping to settle my nerves. I'd done the hard, squeamish part already. I'd sewn up his wound. As the quiet and lack of fighting filled the air around us, my emotions swarmed over me, consuming me with too many thoughts, worries, and questions. Flashbacks of pulling the trigger on Andrey haunted me, and I fidgeted under the enormity of all that had happened.

I was married.

I was a killer.

I would be wanted, already with *one* hit on my head, but damned more so for killing Pavel's son.

"Is this where we will live?" I finished asking. I needed to focus on something, anything, now that I was done concentrating on sewing Alek's shoulder and back wound. If I let this quiet get to me, if I gave in to this idle calm and allowed my mind to wander, I'd go restless and crazy.

"No." He stood, turning to face me.

Without a shirt on, he cut a sharp contrast to my mostly white attire. Strips of the ribbons from my skirts were missing, but only minimal blood marred the shirt he'd given me. His taut skin glowed, tanned and healthy, but the suggestion of his being closer to nudity alerted me to wanting to see—and feel—more.

"I have a few other places." He lifted his hand to tip my chin up, and I blinked at the somber need in his eyes. "We'll find something together. A marital house."

I struggled to swallow, my mouth suddenly dry at the intensity of his stare. We simply gazed at each other as too many unsaid things passed in the air between us.

From him, I saw gratitude, maybe even something like respect or admiration. I wasn't going to wait for him to thank me for saving his life. I had yet to tell him thanks for saving mine, too, and he had in more ways than one. He'd spared me from getting married to an abusive man like his cousin. He'd gotten me away from my father's reach.

If anything, it was I who owed him. Those nerves built and stretched, making me suddenly more anxious and unsettled. He saw the uneasiness in my eyes, and he gripped my elbow, tugging me toward him as he backed us out of the bathroom.

I was his property now. His to move as he wanted, to do with as he pleased.

For the first time, the idea of being his—completely his—thrilled me.

I was Alek's wife, not some used-up virgin he'd taken.

I was his woman.

His other half.

"Remember what I promised?"

I stumbled, looking deep into his dark brown eyes as he led me further from the bathroom and toward what seemed to be a richly decorated yet masculine bedroom. Lights were dimmed low, but I wasn't stumbling in the dark. I reached for him, anyway, hanging my arm around his neck and careful not to touch the tender flesh I'd just sewn up and bandaged.

"You've made no promises," I argued, hoping I sounded playful, not scared.

"You didn't run," he reminded me as he picked up my hand and kissed the spot where my wedding band rested on my finger. "And I told you if you didn't think about running…" He pushed me.

I stepped away slightly, and as the backs of my knees hit the mattress, I lost my balance and tumbled onto the king-size bed. Captured by his smoldering look, I scrambled to sit up and watch him, unable to tear my attention away for a single second.

His fingers made quick work of his pants. He unzipped and lowered his clothes, and his long, hard dick sprang free.

I moaned, so low and quiet, I doubted he could hear, but he saw me rub my thighs together.

"I told you if you didn't run, you could have this."

I exhaled a shaky breath, watching him rub his fist up and down his shaft. Already, the tip leaked drops of precum, and I licked my lips in anticipation.

He was right. I wouldn't have considered it a promise, per se, but he had taunted me and left me unsatisfied in the other apartment. He'd led me on, teased me to a dripping, sex-crazed mess, and aborted seeing me come.

I was more than eager to have him now. If he was offering, I'd take anything to chase away the tumultuous visions filling my mind. Sex would grant me a reprieve from dwelling on the horror of what I'd done.

I'd killed someone. With my actions, I'd instigated more danger. I'd accused him of causing war, but I'd incited it even more by killing Andrey.

I'd made my choice, though, and I would stand by my man. In all his naked, rugged glory.

I stood, stripping as quickly as I could without taking my eyes off him. His dark stare roved up and down me, appreciative and needy until I was naked for him.

Once more, he pushed me until I reclined, and he crawled over me, covering me with his body. He didn't last long, grimacing with the pressure of putting weight on his forearm.

"You'll tear your stitches," I worried aloud, and he growled, gritting his teeth as he realized that same fact. In a quick tuck and roll, he repositioned us. He lay back and dragged me over him, and I followed his lead.

His hot hands touched me everywhere, his fingers tweaking my nipples, his palms cupping my breasts, then my ass and my hips.

He gripped the back of my neck, tugging me down to kiss him hard, and I again followed. His guidance taught me how to move, where to go. I straddled him, instinctively grinding down against his long erection that rubbed my sensitive skin. Each back-and-forth rub I rode over him spread my cream. Slick and sticky, wet and chilled when I moved back, I showed us both how aroused I was for him.

"Ride me, Wife."

I opened and closed my mouth, ready to tell him I didn't know how. But it was a lie I couldn't voice aloud. This would be my first time on top, but deep inside, charged with a flaming need to sink down on him, my body knew. I would figure it out with his instructions.

I snagged my lower lip between my teeth and scooted back to grip him. All the veins teased me, enticing me to explore this first touch of my hand on his cock. The texture intrigued me, so hard yet soft, like steel covered with velvet, but he wasn't a patient teacher.

"Fuck me, Mila. Right now." He dug his fingers into my hips as he directed me to line his cockhead to my pussy.

I moaned at the dragging friction of his dick over my clit, and I considered prolonging this exquisite torture. It felt too good. So naughty. I obeyed his order, though, shifting and getting closer to notch the wide, bulbous head to my soaking wet entrance. A few gentle rocks back and forth helped me get a stable stance over him, and I sank down just a bit to let him spear into me that far and stretch me open.

"Oh…" I leaned my head back, craning my neck as the tingles of pleasure streaked up my body. From the tension in my womb to the aching peaks of my nipples, I felt on fire and sizzling.

"Fuck me, *Wife*," he ordered. He wasn't going to wait. Even though he'd insisted that I get on top so he wouldn't injure himself any further, he took over. His fingers clutched at my skin with a punishing grip that would bruise. Holding on to my hips, he held me in place to thrust his cock deeper inside me.

"Alek!" I cried out, half from shock and half from overwhelming excitement. That rough shove into my cunt felt damned good. He was just so thick, so big, and the feeling of being crammed full with his dick thrilled me.

"Fuck me. Now."

I sank down, letting my knees slide over the mattress and widen my opening to him. Shivering and trembling, I lowered until he was seated all the way inside me. I stared at him, reveling in the tortured look of need in his eyes. After a brief moment to catch my breath at this deeper angle, I lifted up and sank back down on him.

I wasn't graceful as I learned my rhythm, but eventually, as I followed the cues from my body and the intense pressure of the orgasm I chased, I figured it out.

He held my hips, urging me to ride him faster and harder, grinding down and rubbing my clit against him. When he lifted his fingers to that hard bud of need, he helped me get there further. Every filthy word he said pushed me toward letting go, and when I did, crying out and clenching around his jerking dick as he came with me, bursts of light sparkled behind my closed lids.

I was a trembling, quivering mess of bliss, almost dizzy from the force of my release, but he didn't let me fall.

Gathering me in his arms, he pulled me down until I lay draped over him. And with his steady heartbeat thudding beneath my cheek, I rested my head on his chest and surrendered to the lure of sleep.

23

ALEK

Three more times, late into the night, I fucked my wife.

My wife.

I didn't know if or when that phrase would stop getting to me. I'd never thought I'd get married. I would've been content to be a bachelor and remain unattached for the rest of my life.

Now that I was married, I couldn't get enough of that phrase.

My wife. I was addicted to the fact that she was mine. Mine to possess, to fuck, to protect. Mila was sworn to me, and I would never forget it.

As she slept in, well into the morning on the day after our wedding, I sighed and let her catch up on her rest. I'd worn her out all night long, making good on showing her how hot it could be between us. The chemistry sizzling between us was an unstoppable force. All it took was one heated look, one delicate brush of her skin against mine, and I wanted her again.

The wound stretching over my shoulder and onto my back held me back from taking her as roughly as I wanted, but we still made it work.

I worked *her*. Bouncing on my dick with her tits jiggling. On her hands and knees as I pounded into her from behind. Then fucking her pretty mouth before I ate her sweet cunt again.

In the quiet of the morning after, I thought back to how else she'd blown my mind.

At that office complex, she hadn't hesitated to rush in and save me. When I'd tried and failed to twist and reach for my gun, she'd taken care of it. She had the courage and bravery to fire my gun at Andrey for the sake of saving my life, and I would never forget her sacrifice. For me.

My brothers and fellow soldiers wouldn't have hesitated. But Mila? I felt like it was a prudent chore to dissect why she would feel the same loyalty to the man who'd kidnapped her.

She chose to save me, to marry me, and now that I had a chance to think without lust ruling my dick and mind, I wondered about her motives. Sure, she wanted me, but she wasn't a brainless, sex-addicted idiot who'd obey her body over her mind. She was intelligent.

Can she really care? This much?

It seemed too soon. We hadn't known each other for long, and the time we'd shared was peppered with violence and antagonism. Until I kidnapped her from her wedding, we were enemies, children of rival bratvas.

Or is she up to something?

I was too jaded to just trust her, and it annoyed me that I wanted to. Lowering my guard would be a huge mistake. I'd married her, but it seemed trust would need to be earned again and again until the concept penetrated my brain.

Instead of lying there and letting my shoulder and back ache further, I got up and stretched to work the skin into moving again. I was tender and sore, but I would live.

Thanks to you.

I glanced back at her sleeping in the bed, trying to harden my heart to her.

After I dressed, I went through the folded papers Maxim had given me. I didn't learn anything I hadn't already guessed or known. The Kastavas were setting up the Valkovs with this first big shipment received at their Colver dock. As I read through the lines of coded abbreviations and terms, I saw how clearly they wanted to stage this as a sting. It was obviously a setup so they could take over our turf.

My first thought was that another Family could be helping the Kastavas. We had many enemies and rivals, but no one entity came to mind.

The Ortez Cartel was a serious contender, but they wouldn't want to work *with* another bratva to bring us down.

The Italians... I rubbed my jaw, thinking back to how Ivan and I caught that Rossini spy at our warehouse. They were too small now. The Rossinis were weaker from their losses due to infighting.

I wished I could be sure. If I could figure out who this "Doc" was supposed to reference, because I felt certain that once I figured out who that identity belonged to, I would be able to pinpoint this third party who would be involved with this setup.

Reviewing the papers left me in a sour mood, and when Mila woke up, looking rested and so gorgeous as my thoroughly fucked wife, I failed to keep from directing my attitude toward her.

"It's fucking bullshit," I said as I paced, letting her watch me in my fury. "The Kastavas are trying to set us up."

"I'm sorry," she said quietly. It didn't sound like she was apologizing for any fault of her own, but merely sympathizing.

I had no right to be mad at *her*. She hadn't started this. Her father did. Still, she represented the enemy, and my thoughts got twisted and kinked in a nasty knot that left me unsure what to believe or think.

"Where do your allegiances lie?" I demanded. She was my wife now. She belonged to me. But I wondered, nonetheless. I'd never shaken all of my suspicions about her. She came from the enemy, and she had to have something lurking back there in her mind or heart about her family.

"With you, Alek. My husband. Haven't I made that clear by killing Andrey when he wanted to end your life?"

"Did you marry me to be a spy? Was that why you wanted to marry me?"

She stood, narrowing her eyes with fury as she wrapped the sheet around her body. "Why I wanted to? Don't you dare talk to me like that. Like I had a choice in any of this!"

"Why did you want to marry me?" She had to have a motive beneath it all. "What are you really after?"

"Nothing!" She fisted her hand and shoved it low to her side. "Nothing, Alek! I was never allowed to want anything. I knew better than to ever have a fucking dream."

I stared at her panting and seething after her outburst.

"My father ordered me to marry Andrey. *You* took charge, kidnapping me. Then when I was tied up and bound, you gave me no choice but to go along and marry you!" She stabbed her finger at her chest. "I've never been allowed to make my own choices."

I stepped up close, hardening my heart to the sight of tears building in her eyes. "You did. You could have run, but you chose to marry me."

"Because standing with you was the smart way forward."

Smart? I wondered at her choice of words. "Did you marry me to be a spy?"

"For *whom?*" she sobbed, losing her composure. "Who the hell would I be a spy for? My father? He wishes me dead!"

She spoke the truth, but I refused to let her tears sway me. I knew she was telling the truth. The women in the bratva world had no real futures. They called no shots and were not trusted with any lasting decisions. I almost softened to the sound of her crying as she slumped back to sit on the edge of the bed, but I refused to be that moved and gullible.

All my life, I'd been exposed to deceit and liars, and I refused to be stupid now. Even with my wife.

I grabbed a jacket and picked up my phone and gun. I felt her tracking my movements, but I didn't do more than glance at her as I bade her farewell. "I'm going to speak with my brothers." I pointed at her tear-streaked face. "Don't think about leaving. The building is guarded and watched by men loyal to me."

She lowered her face, glancing down and away as she sniffled louder.

And with her tears dripping to the sheets, I strode out into the hall-way, slamming the door shut behind me.

If only I could slam the door to the wall guarding my heart, too, then all would be right in my world.

I wasn't supposed to… care. Love wasn't in the cards in this hard life. It was a weakness, a distraction, but she tormented me to consider that it could be building between us regardless.

24

MILA

The door slammed shut, and I flinched at the loud bang. Just like that, Alek stormed out of here, leaving me like some thing to ignore. When the going got tough…

Stop. I sighed a watery exhale and wiped my face. Tears smeared a hot trail of liquid over my cheeks, and I loathed that he'd pushed me to lose my composure like this. I *never* cried, never broke down, no matter how hard life would treat me, but he'd gone too far.

What else can I fucking do?

I shot and killed a man to save him. I chose to marry him and gave up the idea of running to my freedom away from the criminal world we orbited in.

And still, he didn't trust me.

He'd looked at me with such scathing hatred, assuming *I* was the bad guy out to get him. That I was working on screwing him over like some ultra-secret femme fatale.

I huffed and rolled my eyes. It was so ridiculous that I almost giggled, but I was too upset to loosen up and laugh off his reaction.

I wasn't shocked that he'd be jaded and quick to assume the worst of me. I wouldn't have been surprised if he hadn't guessed at my motive. Alek had lived a hard life rife with manipulation and frustration. He wasn't a gentle soul, and he was raised to be a hard asshole. But for fuck's sake, I was too damned confused to understand how he'd switched his moods so suddenly from last night.

Just who did he think I would be spying for? My father who wanted me dead?

I couldn't make sense of it. I'd woken up with a teeny, tenuous thread of hope. As my eyes opened to a new day, I started to think that we were building something real here, something far more than just fucking or arranging power plays.

Now, he was only proving to be just like Andrey or my father, all the other men I'd met in my life—out for himself and never letting anyone in.

Pushing to my feet, I fought for a moment of strength. I was determined to stay positive. Because this was to be expected, right? This was the way my life was destined to play out—as the object of a man's wishes.

As I went to the bathroom and began to clean up and shower, I wondered how much worse Alek might treat me. If he wanted to start the first day of our lives together in a fight, what would it escalate to in the future?

Just as I was warming up to him and enjoying how he could push me and coax me to surrendering to his brand of brutal pleasure, making me feel so pretty and sexy and wanted, not fat or undesirable, he had to change into an asshole again.

After I showered and dried off, I went through his clothes to find the smallest garments that would cover me. I had no clothes. I had *nothing* and no one here, but I couldn't know when I could expect anything delivered to me.

I may as well be grateful that he forgot to tie me up again. I huffed, irked by my bitter thoughts as I left the bedroom.

I didn't know what to do, but I refused to sit around and wait for him to return. That much idle downtime would wreak havoc on my mind. So, I got up and tried to keep myself as busy as possible. Tidying the apartment felt like I was intruding and invading someone else's space, but I dusted and sorted out the minimal clutter throughout the apartment. When I finished that, dismayed that it had only lasted an hour, I knew I was too antsy to sit again.

Bored and restless with all my thoughts, I moved into the kitchen and checked the contents at hand. I could start on a meal. Lunch was soon, but if he needed more time to stew and put distance between us, it could be dinner. Even if we ended up leaving this place and staying somewhere else, it would be a productive way to while away the minutes or hours until he'd want to return.

Just as I reached into the fridge for the container of chicken in the far back spot on the shelf, I heard the door open.

"How does—"

Arms wrapped around me, cutting me off from announcing my thoughts about food. The muscled limbs held me tight, but it felt all wrong. *He* was wrong. This masked intruder didn't smell like my husband, all spicy and clean with his familiar musky scent beneath. He wasn't as tall as my ruggedly fit spouse.

This man was too rough, shoving me against the counter as he wrenched me away from the fridge.

His gloved hand slapped over my mouth, cutting off my scream. Worse, though, was the immediate shove of his other hand. He pushed it under my pants, trying to remove my garments.

"Playing housewife now?" he growled into my ear as he gripped me hard, digging his nails along the upper skin of my thighs.

My pulse skyrocketed with the instant thunder of my heartbeat.

Geoff. I recognized his voice. I recalled that filthy, sinister tone when he'd try to get his way with me. Of all the people to sneak in here and attack me, he was the last one I ever wanted to see or hear of again.

Rage built within me, and I lashed out, wrestling and wiggling to break free. My fight encouraged him to grab my pussy harder. I cried out at the intrusive, painful touch, but that noise was just the reward he was looking for. My agony was music to his sick ears. He chuckled, low and evil, as though my reaction was a perfect present for the sadist he was.

"It's about time that I got my hands on you," he taunted.

I bucked back at him, trying to escape the way he pinned me to the counter. He was taller and stronger, and he acted on years of pent-up obsession over me. He would never release me. I was doomed, alone and without a weapon in this place.

I didn't want to think of how he'd gotten in here. Alek said it was guarded. I saw the cameras and patrolmen on the way here. It was a protected fortress, but still, Geoff had gotten in.

If he'd gone to that much trouble to reach me, he wouldn't quit for anything.

Like hell, I'll let him have his way with me!

Desperate and panicked, I bit down hard on his gloved hand over my mouth, triumphant when my teeth cut through the leather and pierced his skin.

"You bitch!" He lowered his hand and shook it, then yanked off his mask. "It's me. Don't fucking bite me."

"I know who you are," I shot back. As if recognizing that he was one of my father's men would make me behave. Knowing he was associated with my father made me more livid, not the opposite.

He gripped my hair, yanking my head back as he swore and shoved faster at my pants. "Then you know that you'd better listen good. Give me those papers."

His breath came out in rushed exhales as he struggled to keep me captive and lower his pants.

Papers? I didn't understand.

"I need that information your *husband*"—he snarled the word with disgust—"was given at your fucking wedding. Where is it?"

The folded papers? I'd barely realized what they were when Maxim handed them to Alek. I spotted those lines of code, but I'd been stuck in panic mode for killing Andrey. I hadn't considered them again, not until Geoff spoke now.

I didn't want to know how he could be aware of them. Spies and espionage were commonplace in our world. Anything could be tracked or trailed. Maybe that man Alek sent back to Pavel had spoken too soon or somewhere that Kastava soldiers could have listened in. There were many ways that Geoff or my father's men could have learned about Maxim giving Alek secretive intel. All that mattered now was that Geoff did know, and he was planning to use me to gain that information for himself.

I bucked and twisted, fighting him until my last breath. If he dared to touch what wasn't his, if he tried to fit where only Alek belonged...

No. I screamed, clawing to get free.

"I need that intel, bitch. Where is it?"

"Fuck those papers! And fuck you!" A hard elbow jab to his side almost won me freedom, but he resisted with a grunt and held me tighter. My scalp burned with the tighter clench of his fingers in my hair, and tears streaked from my eyes.

"No, I'll fuck *you*, bitch. Your father should have given you to me. Even if you're damaged goods now, you can serve me. Serve your

Family and do your duty. You'll give me those papers right after I fuck this pussy."

I set my teeth together so hard that my jaw strained from the effort. Ugly, dark fury filled me at the reminder that according to him, to my father, to all the men in the world, I would always be something to use. To dispose of.

"I won't be a spy." I slapped my hand out, gripping the closest thing on the counter as he tried to spread my legs apart.

His chest heaved at my back as he forced me to bend over so he could rape me. "The fuck you won't."

"I won't be a pawn in this war." I narrowed my eyes as he slammed my head to the counter, forcing my ass into the air. I saw red even as in my mind, I wished Alek were here to save me.

He wasn't, though. And it was, again, up to me to save the day.

I grabbed the handle to the knife I'd planned to use for preparing a meal, but instead, I aimed it at Geoff. He lost his hold on me as I twisted at the hips. Before he could shove himself inside me, I reached low and gripped his dick hard—then I sliced it off with one hard, forceful hacking motion.

He released me, screaming and falling back, and I ran.

I didn't stop to check whether he would chase me. I didn't slow to grab shoes.

As he screeched and let out morbid wails of pain and rage in the kitchen, I sprinted out the still-open door and ran like my life depended on it.

25

ALEK

I didn't go far from Mila. A couple of blocks down the street, my men waited in the basement level of a warehouse. Office suites had been renovated down here, and it was where my brothers and several other soldiers stood around and paced. Hiding and working in the shadows offered no pride, but until we took over, we would operate however we could. We weren't cowards, tiptoeing around Pavel and his men, but rather, cautious men at war.

I called them my men because they were. My brothers would always stand by me. These others were loyal to the Family, not Pavel himself.

Ivan and Dmitri nodded at me in greeting, and I went to stand with Nikolai and Maxim. He'd been treated. He had to have been, because he looked much better than he had the day before.

"Where is your wife?" he asked as I sat on a stool.

I'd already texted them to have one of our medics in attendance. I trusted Mila's stitches on my back and shoulder, but it wouldn't hurt to have another look at it.

"Resting," I replied curtly. The truth was that I'd stormed away from her, bothered by how much I wanted to let her in and feel for her. Emotions like that would be my downfall.

"Hmm." Ivan shared a glance with Nik, who failed to hide a smile.

Never mind that now. I didn't come here to hear them give me shit or tease me about why and how I would have made her so tired as to need to rest up this late into the day.

I shot them a stern look, hoping that a breather from her would lend me more clarity of mind.

"Who stitched you up?" the medic asked as he pushed my shirt further off my shoulder to look at the wound.

"Mila," I replied, then cleared my throat. I glanced around the room, lifting my chin as a gesture of approval. They understood that I wanted an update, not to be asked how Mila and I were getting along.

"Pavel is furious," a soldier said. "He has been led to believe that you shot Andrey."

I nodded. *Just as I wanted.*

"He's sworn revenge. He's placed a hit out for you." The man glanced around at the rest of us. "And we are all keeping tabs on the soldiers he's sending out to make that happen."

"I appreciate it," I replied solemnly.

"You will lead us, Aleksei," another said. A few others chorused the same sentiment, promising their loyalty to me and that they would follow my directions.

"It was a long time coming," someone else claimed. If anything, these men respected me more for believing that I'd killed Andrey. They weren't upset at losing the supposed heir to the bratva. Instead, they held me in a higher esteem for seeing the dirty work done.

I reiterated the need for caution, and they explained how they were also watching the Colver dock and tailing select members of the Kastava force.

"They want to set us up," Nikolai said. "They want to take us over with the shipment."

"But who is helping them?" Maxim asked. "I've looked over those codes several times, and I just don't understand."

I do. On the walk over here, I pieced it together. "The cops."

"Well, yes," Ivan said. "They will set us up to take the fall for that arms shipment. And the law enforcement will be on us like never before with a shipment that large."

"Not that large," Maxim argued. "Pavel never had enough to fund as large of a shipment as he boasted."

"Regardless, the cops will be there when it falls apart," Nik argued.

"Which cop?" Dmitri asked, realizing how confident and calm I was. He knew I was on to something.

"Did Mila explain it to you?" Nik asked. "She was working in that office. Their front company."

I'd dismissed that connection. Sergei never would have directly trusted her with any vital clues. I shook my head.

"But can she help? Can she give us any information?"

I tensed. "My wife is not a pawn to use."

They didn't speak up, hesitant at my dark tone.

"She has no information to give me," I said, knowing then and there that it had to be true. If she had anything to share, she would have. She couldn't go at this halfway. How could she want to save my life but not help me win this war?

"I don't need any more information. I've got it all. We have it all." With the medic finished inspecting my wound, I tugged my shirt and jacket back on then retrieved the papers from my inner pocket.

It had taken me too long to realize it, but rereading the coded lines over and over helped me piece it together.

"The Doc," I said.

"As in the *dock*?" Maxim guessed. "Referencing the Colver dock that we want from the Kastavas?"

I shook my head. "No. As in the former doctor. The 'Doc.'"

No one reacted, and I turned to Nikolai. He was most used to this specialty, used to going undercover on assignments. "Remember that rookie who moved up in ranks because he disguised himself as a physician to get closer to his targets on cases?"

He snapped his fingers and cursed. "That fucker."

"Who?" Ivan asked.

"Stephen Murphy. That fucking two-timing cop. I remember him."

"He's involved?" Dmitri asked.

I nodded. Rereading those clues within the emails Maxim intercepted was all it took to jog my memory. Stephen Murphy had always been a thorn in our side. All the cops and detectives wanted to bring the bratva down, and he was the sneakiest of the bunch. He'd once snuck in undercover at a prison, pretending to be a doctor, to get a statement from one of the men the bratva had nearly killed. It was a nasty case of he said versus they said, and on and on, and since that time, everyone knew he would never be trusted.

"Then what are we waiting for?" Ivan asked.

I shook my head. We had to do this right. If Murphy or any other cop was trying to help Sergei Kastava set us up, we had to be just as sneaky and careful with getting them back. "We're not *waiting*. We're planning."

And we did. With these dozen or so loyalists, I schemed and strategized how to fight back. Nikolai and Maxim worked on the laptop, hacking into surveillance software to find where this asshole cop might be. We'd already put a tracker on Pavel and Sergei, too.

The rest of us tried to think of how we could change the details of the shipment's arrival so the Kastavas wouldn't screw us over. Their men and soldiers would have to be at the dock. They would man the crews unloading the goods, but the transportation of the arms from the docks to the warehouse was where the trap would be set. The cops couldn't find the Valkovs at fault there, but instead, Sergei's men.

For another hour, we deliberated the best method to make sure we wouldn't be taken down with the blame for this scenario. If anyone was going to be caught by the law with one of the biggest North American arms shipments ever, it wouldn't be us.

The longer I stayed apart from Mila, the more I began to consider that I could trust my gut with her. I didn't want to think that I was missing her. Not already. We'd been thrust together with such close proximity for so long now that it felt weird to be apart from her.

But she's not the enemy. She had no choice in being born a Kastava, but through marriage, I'd helped her fix her identity. She was a Valkov now. She was mine.

And I felt closer to being ready to trust her.

She hadn't once asked to see those papers. She hadn't said or acted in any other suspicious manner.

Most importantly, she saved my life. I had to give her credit and seriously start to think that she might want to be on my side without any nefarious plans lurking behind her eyes.

"Alek?" Dmitri walked up closer, holding his finger up to get my attention. "I've got a bead on Murphy." He put his phone back in his pocket and nodded.

I knew it wouldn't take long. Other than these men in here, more were out there working the streets. More yet were guarding the building where I'd left my wife crying on the bed.

Enough. I can make it up to her later.

"Let's go." It was about time someone located the cop referenced ambiguously as "The Doc" in those coded and encrypted emails. "I'll come with you to... talk to him."

Because the faster we put *our* trap in place to screw over our rivals, the sooner I could go home and address my wife.

Acting on this war would make me feel better. I would feel productive, like I was accomplishing something. All this time since I'd instigated this war and shaken things up, I'd been hiding, lurking and keeping Mila out of anyone's reach.

Her safety was paramount. She was my priority, my future, but in the meantime, I could be the leader I was born to be. I would show these men, my men, how Pavel had failed to guide us.

A real leader would go out in the warzone and handle battles himself.

Dmitri got into the driver's side of a car parked out back, but he waited to turn the key.

"What's wrong?" I asked as he reached into his jacket.

"I went through Pavel's safe like you'd asked."

I frowned.

Nikolai joined us, sliding into the backseat.

"You told me to search for Father's things. To find Mother's ring to give to Mila before you married her," Dmitri said.

197

"And we couldn't find shit. I thought he'd burned it all or something," Nik added from the back. "Until I thought to look in his safe."

"He broke into it," Dmitri said. "We didn't find the ring, or anything of Father's, except this." His expression was guarded and sorrowful, almost as though he didn't want to show me what this paper would reveal.

I took the document, realizing it was actually a pair of them. The first was Pavel's birth certificate. The other was our father's. They were twins. We all knew that, and as such, there was nothing to question. They were legitimate sons of our grandparents. Not bastards.

I shrugged.

"The times," Nik advised.

I looked again. Then again. Back and forth, I tracked my eyes over the numbers that couldn't lie.

Pavel wasn't the firstborn twin.

My father, Pyotr Valkov, was.

Which meant Andrey had never been the actual heir to the bratva.

I am.

I slammed my fist to the dashboard, furious at my uncle's deception.

"All the more reason to finish this business," I said, letting my ire leak through my words.

Because he's next. And he'll be the last to ever try to ruin the truth as I know it.

26

MILA

I ran out of the apartment and nearly skidded to a rough stop against the wall. A guard lay dead on the hallway floor, a bullet neatly embedded between his eyes.

Geoff had killed him. He had to have. There was no other explanation for it, but I knew that man was too far gone.

I couldn't stall. Stopping or hesitating would be a grave mistake. With Geoff wounded and furious in the apartment, he'd been eager to chase me down. I had no way of guessing whether he had backup, where others from my father's force could be hiding or waiting, or if anyone here would help me.

If Alek could question himself and give evidence of not being able to fully trust me because I was a Kastava, would his men?

I ran all the way out to the streets. Being in the open helped me beat back the gnawing claustrophobia that had overtaken me in the hallways as I fled the scene, but on the streets again, I felt more vulnerable. My father's men could be out here. Alek's could too. It seemed that no matter where I looked or what I did, enemies would always be lurking too close.

Who can I trust? Where can I go?

Rain fell from the skies, and with a chilly gust of air cutting down the street, I was instantly chilled by more than just fear.

I shielded my face as I dared a look back. No one ran after me, but a phantom sense of feeling that I was being chased kept me running from the building. I couldn't hear anyone running after me. No one popped up and tried to grab me, but the terror remained under my skin, propelling me to hurry away.

I had no sense of direction. Deep in this Valkov territory, I was lost and unaware of my surroundings. All I knew was to keep running and seek somewhere to hide. Three times, I almost ran out at intersections. People shouted and horns blared, but I dismissed it all and kept going. If I stayed mobile, it would be harder to be caught.

Time fell away from me, and I grew colder and wearier without a clue of how long I'd run for, much less where I was going.

I had no one to call for help. Alek hadn't given me a phone, and I wouldn't have known his number, anyway. My father wasn't a source of help, either. He wanted me dead. Rosamund might have been the closest thing to a person I could consider a friend, but she wasn't within reach, either.

I had nothing and no one, and I fought back tears with how badly I wished I could have Alek with me.

He'd protected me so far. I felt confident that he would again. I had so much to learn about him, but I knew somehow that he was a man of his word. When he married me, he'd meant it.

"Hey!"

I regretted that I'd slowed to a walk. My lungs burned. My skin was chilled and soaked, and my feet bled from running so hard on the sidewalks barefoot like this.

A pair of beat cops had noticed me, and I knew they wouldn't give up. I hadn't dressed for the weather, and I was sure my eyes hadn't yet lost that look of pure horror and fear.

"You on the run?" one asked. The other spoke into his radio piece on his coat.

"No." I swallowed, forcing moisture down my dry throat that felt so raw and harsh from the exercise of running hard.

"Easy, Ma'am, easy."

I backed up as they approached.

"We're here to help."

I shook my head. They might think they could, but I knew better. They'd want to know who I belonged to, where I called home, and I couldn't reveal that.

"Ma'am." One lifted his hand. His partner hurried after me as I turned to sprint away again.

A third cop stopped me. He must have been coming to join them on this rainy day, and it was his wide chest that I ran into.

I bounced back from the impact, but he caught my upper arm. His fingers wrapped around the spot where I'd been shot, and I hissed at the contact.

"Are you hurt?" he demanded.

I was. But I refused to speak to them. It was too dangerous. Even if I wasn't a Kastava anymore, I was a Valkov woman now, and no bratva women ever spoke freely with law enforcement. That rule of life had been ingrained in my brain from an early age.

I sagged, caught and kept in place as the cops ganged up around me. Pedestrians didn't notice, keeping their faces down or tucked under umbrellas. They all parted us as we stood in the center of the path, and I prayed that just one of them, anyone, could intervene and help me get away.

I'd been praying for a rescue, but I knew these figures of authority wouldn't save me.

"She's Kastava's daughter," the redheaded cop said. A sneer slid over his face as he looked me up and down. Water beaded and dripped from his auburn facial hair, and he tightened his grip on my arm.

Fuck.

"Guess we should get her back where she belongs," another said as the redheaded man held on tightly.

"No." I swallowed. "I'm not her. I'm no one."

I'm Aleksei Valkov's wife, goddammit!

The scream waited on the tip of my tongue, but I couldn't release it.

As he prompted me to walk with him, I realized he was taking me toward a station that I'd run past. If he brought me in there, I'd have no chance of escape.

I didn't want to go back to my father. That promised death.

I didn't want to be tossed around or held like a prisoner. Once had been enough.

"Murphy, maybe she's right," the other cop argued. "She looks lost."

Murphy? I racked my brain, thinking back to the last time I'd seen that name. I hadn't heard it but read it. Way back when my father asked me to begin forwarding those emails in that wonky cycle of chain emails, that name had been included in the abbreviations and codes. I'd only seen it the one time, and after that, the nickname of *Doc* had been used.

Oh, my God!

It was him. He was the one they were referencing in all those secret emails.

A cop! Those codes and abbreviations were hiding the fact that my father was leaning on the cops to help him take over Alek's family.

My father had gone too far, stooping so low as to work *with* the law enforcement to bring down the Valkov Bratva once and for all. His greed was so severe, an all-consuming drive, that he'd gone to the outside to defeat his enemy.

My heart raced faster as all the details clicked into place. I'd never been told anything concrete, but with the little I knew from managing the fake S.T.L. business, I was aware that a large illegal shipment was due in soon.

When? When is it supposed to happen? I hadn't been at the computer for a few days now, and it seemed like those hours spent in the office could have been years ago. I'd been so nostalgic about being married off because it signaled the end of my service in the office. I'd liked having busywork to do, even though it had been undecipherable.

Tomorrow! I gasped as I realized the timeline of the days that had passed. With my wedding, its abrupt end, then being kidnapped, fucked, and married, enough time had passed that the big shipment was almost here. Whatever my father had machinated against Pavel Valkov, it was going to go down at the Colver dock tomorrow.

I have to tell Alek! I thought again to how Maxim had handed him papers that looked so similar to the emails I'd forwarded. I hadn't thought about them enough, but Maxim must have somehow intercepted it all.

Alek wanted to oust his uncle from power, likely because he had his suspicions about what his uncle and my father were doing, working "together" on this shipment. I doubted Pavel was aware that this dirty cop was also included in that secretive and duplicitous version of teamwork.

It's a setup. No wonder he's been so on guard and edgy with me.

Alek wasn't just jaded, he was sharp and determined to make sure the Valkov Bratva wouldn't be ruined.

The cop tugged me to walk faster. "I said what were you doing out here?"

I hadn't heard him ask me the first time, too busy connecting all the dots.

He didn't deserve the truth from me, and I fought to wrench my arm from his grasp. "Let me go."

He whistled, lifting his head to a man lurking in the shadows near the station's entrance.

I cowered back, afraid to see Lev standing there, like he'd been waiting. He'd probably come as Geoff's backup, waiting in the distance while Geoff tried to get me to heel.

"Fuck." I shook my head, clawing to get away from the cop. "No. Let me go."

"Oh, I'll let you go, all right." He shoved me forward so Lev could capture me.

"I'll let you go right back into the hands of your handlers." The cop chuckled, nodding a greeting to Lev. "Found one of yours."

"No!" I wiggled, fighting to slip free, but Lev tightened his arm around me.

"Thanks, Doc."

I gasped again, knowing without a doubt that this cop was in on the setup.

"Let me go!" I shouted it louder, earning some glances as Lev dragged me down the alley.

"Let me go," I shouted at him as he hauled me through the rain. "I want to go to my husband."

He laughed darkly, pulling his hood lower as he dragged me toward a car parked in the alley.

My life flashed before my eyes again. The second he got me in that car and drove me back to my father, I would be dead. I would get no mercy, no chance to beg for my life. He didn't value me, not for anything, especially after I'd defied him by marrying Alek instead of Andrey.

"He'll be looking for me," I screamed, desperate to return to the man I wanted to help. "My husband will be looking for me!"

"See if I give a fuck."

"Lev, you can't take me back. I don't want to see my father."

He scoffed. "Neither does he. He just wants you dead. Out of the picture, you traitorous bitch."

"Just let me go!"

"No." He shook my arm, moving me to hurry faster to his car. "If you can't serve as a spy the way he wants you to, you're good for nothing!"

Lev grabbed me as I dragged my feet, forcing him to turn and catch me.

He stopped short, lifting his face as we saw we weren't alone in this alleyway.

A murderous glare locked on us.

Alek.

He came! Hope filled me, and I let out a cry of relief just at the sight of him in my darkest, most hopeless moment.

He stood there, cracking his knuckles with the promise of rabid rage in his dark eyes.

Like a premonition of pain, he looked ready to kill.

For me.

27

ALEK

Seeing Mila caught in the grip of Sergei Kastava's top soldier's hands sent me spiraling and sinking into a deep rage unlike anything else I'd ever felt. My arms and legs vibrated with the urgent need to inflict pain, and I let the wrath coat me like a shield.

I exhaled hard through my nostrils for a moment, letting this image etch into my brain. Because this would be the last time. This would be the very last time any man ever dared to touch my woman.

"Let go of my wife," I ordered in a lethal tone that promised no mercy.

"Fuck you," Lev sneered, shoving her to the side with no care for her slipping and falling into a puddle. Hearing her cry out at the rough handling stoked the fire and anger within. I fumed, overwhelmed with the immediate urge to end his life.

"You touch my wife and die," I vowed. I'd slaughter him and slay every other motherfucker who dared to harm a hair on her head.

Mila was mine, and I would burn the goddamn world down for her if I had to.

He lifted his gun to aim it at me, but I wasn't that stupid. I wouldn't rise to his bait. We were right next to the station. Police officers and detectives would be swarming the area. Using guns would ensure that all the cops—including Murphy—would come running and intervene.

Sergei had already worked out some kind of a deal with the law enforcement to set the Valkov Bratva up. They would side with Lev here, not me, and I didn't need to risk any more obstacles to getting Mila back in my arms and to safety.

I charged at Lev instead, knocking his gun to the ground. He hadn't kept a good enough hold on it, and the firearm smacked to the pavement, loosening the silencer he'd attached to it. Instead, he retaliated with his hands and feet, attacking me and wrestling to beat me down, man to man.

He wouldn't win. There was no way I would slip and let him get on me like this. Seeing him being rough with Mila ensured that he would receive every ounce of my anger, and I vented it all with every punch, jab, and kick I rained down on his body and face. This was rage, no holds barred. I unleashed a steady stream of violence until he panted and shook, struggling to rise to both knees. He couldn't keep going, worn from the battery of my fists.

A dark mist of violence had claimed my mind, and I wouldn't stop until he'd lost his last breath.

"You touch her, you die," I reminded him as I grabbed his head and twisted hard.

A final, sickening crack followed the gesture. His body went limp, sagging in my hands before I released him with a shove. Over and down, he folded and sank to the puddles in the alley.

I stood there catching my breath from the bloody and brutal fight to the death, staring down at his corpse as I waited for my heart to return to a normal, steadier pace. I wouldn't be calm for another year, it seemed. My heart still charged fast, riled up from seeing Mila targeted and captured to be returned to her father.

Still, I'd heard her beg to be released. Flashbacks of her cries replayed in my mind, when she'd demanded that Lev release her. Her warnings that I'd be out looking for her and wanting her back.

She was right. And wrong.

Dmitri and I had been coming here to corner Murphy and spy on him for the sake of changing the details of tomorrow's big shipment coming in to the Colver dock.

As soon as he'd parked nearby, I got a call reporting the deaths of three guards at the building, all shot dead by none other than Geoff Federov. Cameras had caught him breaking in and trying to rape my wife in our home.

The second I heard her crying out in the alley, I'd run back here, ensuring Dmitri could leave to deal with the chaos at the building.

It's done. He's dead. He can't hurt her. I heaved out one more deep breath and turned to see her where she'd snuck back to hide alongside a dumpster. Soaking wet, she looked drenched and miserable. I saw her shaking from the cold as I stalked over to her. Her hair was plastered to her head, and as I neared her, she stared up at me with wide-open, trusting but fearful eyes. Unsteadily, she rose to her feet, but she didn't take her hands from her ears. She'd no doubt covered them at the awful sound of Lev's neck snapping.

"Come here." I didn't order it harshly despite the rage still simmering in my blood. I offered her my hand, trying to coax her closer.

She came. She stepped carefully toward me, lowering her hands to take the one I held out to her.

The moment she placed her delicate fingers, so icy cold and wet, in my hand, I grabbed her close and wrapped my arms around her.

She sobbed, shivering, shuddering, and sniffling against me. I felt every tremor of her body shaking in the cold and fear, and I didn't waste a second to scoop her into my arms and carry her further from the man who'd tried to return her to her father against her wishes.

"I… I…"

I pressed a kiss to her temple as she tucked her face to me, burrowing close.

"I didn't run."

I barked out a single laugh. Nothing about this was humorous, but still. "You did."

"I ran to hide." She cried harder, then cleared her throat harshly, as though she scolded herself to stay strong. "I ran to get away from him and I didn't… I didn't know where you were."

That's the last time we'll ever make that mistake. "I know."

"I'm sorry. Alek, I didn't… I didn't run."

I kissed her again, clutching her closer as I brought her to the car.

Dmitri had already come back. I saw his car pulling up at the end of the alley, and he didn't utter a word as he got out and opened the back door for us. I climbed in, not releasing my grip on her once as I adjusted her on my lap.

My brother knew better than to speak as he drove. When I met his gaze in the reflection of the rearview mirror, he nodded once.

I interpreted that as the all-clear. He'd handled Geoff's corpse at the apartment. He'd seen to the removal of all the bodies and blood.

I nodded back, knowing he would understand and receive my thanks in that silent gesture.

Words weren't necessary now. All that mattered was making sure

Mila was warm and clean, safe and dry. And with me, where she belonged.

I hated that I'd let my doubts get the better of me this morning. As she trembled and cried softly in my lap, I vowed to never doubt her again. I'd suspected that she was a rare gift, a unique and unlikely gift that I wasn't sure I deserved. I had a hunch deep down inside that she was worthy of my trust, and I despised that it had taken me so long to get my head out of my ass and realize it.

Dmitri drove us home, still without a word, and I carried Mila up to our apartment. A quick glance showed me that the cleaners had done their jobs with excellence. Nothing looked out of place, and not a speck of blood remained in the halls or the apartment. Sometimes, waterproof backing and liners for carpet was all the world needed to be restored to normal with speed.

I lowered her to her feet in the bathroom. As she sensed me getting ready to release her, she curled her fingers tighter in my shirt, not wanting to let me go.

"Where... How..." She swallowed, wincing at the motion. "What happened to the... men?"

"They've been disposed of."

She blinked, nodding as I began to strip her clothes from her trembling, icy-to-touch body.

"Geoff broke in." She swallowed again, staring at me with such a vacant look that I doubted she was focusing on me at all but looking through me. That blank void she wore suggested she was reliving the horrors she'd survived without my help, and I would never forgive myself for her suffering without me there to save her.

"He..." She shook harder as I turned the shower on. "He broke in and tried to rape me. He said even though I was damaged goods, he still wanted to have me. All my life, he's tried to rape me, to take what wasn't his. He was obsessed, and I refused to live in fear of him for another moment."

She spoke faster, gaining confidence or anger as she rambled, unaware that I was stripping her to warm her in the shower.

"He wanted the papers that Maxim gave you at the wedding. I'd forgotten about them. I was so stunned that I'd killed someone. That I'd killed your cousin. An heir. I was so stuck in the shock that I didn't realize at first that your brother had copies of emails from Kastava sources. My father used to request that I transfer them. In the office, I was supposed to forward all those coded things and pass them along to different addresses." She licked her lips, nodding as she rambled, almost with a panicked rush.

"He ordered me to report to him after I married Andrey," she rushed to add as I guided her backward into the shower.

Her skin bore the marks of a struggle, but she wasn't wounded too badly despite her scuffles with Geoff, then Lev and the cops. She winced at the first hit of hot water on her flesh, but I knew it had to be the shock of heat on her chilled skin. Her smooth flesh would return to normal. I wasn't worried about hypothermia, but rather, shock.

I held her hands, ensuring she didn't trip in the trancelike fugue she moved with as she stepped under the water, still facing me through the open door.

"He wanted me to still answer to him," she added, gazing at me with such open sincerity that I knew she needed me calm.

I nodded, letting her know I listened as I removed my wet clothes.

"He said I was to serve him and never hesitate to answer to him, but I didn't. I wouldn't. He wants me dead, and I never want to return to him."

I entered the shower, joining her under the pelting water. She clung to me, wrapping her arms around me and tucking her face to my chest as her emotions got to her once more.

Holding her tightly, I tried to warm her up and calm her from this frantic spill of her fears and worries.

"Geoff wanted me to give him papers so they would have intel about that big shipment, but I didn't know where they were. Even if I did, I wouldn't have ever helped him, Alek. I am your wife, your partner, and I will choose you."

I cupped her face and tipped it up to kiss her lips. Desire warred with my need to comfort her, but I didn't plunder her mouth and demand a taste. I kept it simple, bushing my lips over hers with as much tender gentleness as I could manage as I held her tightly.

"I understand." And I did. I understood that now. Mila wouldn't betray me. Not like my uncle had, not like any enemy might want to.

"I was so scared, so worried when Geoff entered. Not only because he wanted to rape me, but because I thought you would assume I'd called him here, that I asked him to find me. And Lev. I didn't know he was nearby, potentially waiting to bring me to my father."

"I saw it on the video," I said calmly, stroking her long, brown locks back from her face as she blinked up at me.

"You did?"

I shook my head. I personally hadn't watched the footage yet. My men had reported it all back to me. I wasn't sure whether I could stomach watching the live-action evidence of when my wife was almost captured, raped, and taken from me. We'd only just found each other. We'd only just married and made our commitment to a future together, and it was far too soon to imagine losing her.

A lifetime with her wouldn't be enough.

I wanted forever.

"They told me."

"He came in and shot a guard," she added, furrowing her brows. Her words left her lips slower now, calmer, as though the rambling rush had soothed her enough to think and take her time speaking.

"Not just one. Three. Geoff killed my men all the way to get to you."

"So they would have protected me?"

I narrowed my eyes. "What do you mean?"

"I worried that maybe since you struggled to trust me and know that I stand by you, your men would fail to follow orders to keep me safe as well."

I shook my head. "They heed my orders. You are my wife." I kissed her harder. "My queen. And they will protect you when I can't."

"I'm sorry." She lowered her gaze but didn't stay cowardly for long. She tipped her chin up and faced me again. "I'm sorry they were killed. I ran out and saw the man dead at the door, and I ran because I didn't know where I would be safe. In here, on the streets, anywhere."

And I'll never leave you without a means of reaching me ever again. This was all new to me. I'd had lovers before, but not a partner, an equal, a wife. I had to consider not only my own safety and survival, but that she'd rely on it too.

"Those cops found me, and it clicked. Those codes in those emails, in those copies that Maxim handed you, they made sense. That day that you and Nik came to the office asking about a Doc, I realized that the Valkovs were included on that shipment correspondence. But I didn't know what anything meant, what would happen. But that cop—"

I grabbed her hand and kissed her fingertips. "I know. The Doc. Stephen Murphy. It's an old, coded nickname that I should have realized sooner."

"He's setting up the bratva," she exclaimed, licking her lips and eager to share all she had learned. "You need to know that he's planning to help somehow. Or something. I don't know, but he's dirty, and my father is working with him!"

I stared into her expressive blue eyes, so open and eager to persuade me to believe her. It wouldn't take much. She spoke of things I had already figured out, and with the fact that she was spilling it all so freely with the intention of helping me and looking out for me and my bratva, I knew she was my woman in every way I needed her to be. Not only my wife, but also my support to lead and take care of the bratva, of the Family.

It was this freely given admission that made me realize once and for all that she was in this with me. She was all in.

"I'll never be a pawn for any man ever again, Alek, but I swear on my life, I will be an agent in seeing to your success, to *our* future."

I clutched her close and kissed her hard, reveling in every sweep of her tongue alongside mine and each breathy moan of need she uttered as she warmed under my touch.

"I trust you, Mila."

I wanted to, and I knew without a doubt that she would never let me regret it.

28

MILA

He held me close, flush against his slippery, warm body. The contact of his hard strength heated me all the way to the marrow of my bones, and I wanted to snuggle up even closer and never let go.

Alek was more than just a spouse. We'd arranged our marriage for the purpose of securing a better future. We were born from rivals, trained to view the other as an enemy above all else. Forging a union between us was the unlikeliest solution to this war we were thrust into, a scrimmage between our bratva leaders, but in it, we'd found so much more.

He was my rock, my anchor.

He was the one who'd save me, protect me, and now, trust me.

I couldn't hold a grudge against him for how long it had taken him to get to this point.

In another world, I should've been quick to demand that he trust me the moment I killed for him. Under any other circumstances, I should have insisted that he declare his trust and loyalty to me—or realize mine for him—the moment I stopped Andrey from shooting him dead.

Alek and I didn't have an ideal beginning. We hadn't started a "normal" relationship by any stretch of the imagination.

We'd met with our guards up, stuck in our positions to view the other as nothing but the opposition.

And in these torrid days of sex, danger, and lies, we'd come together to be stronger and wiser.

"And I love you, Alek," I said solemnly, staring straight into his eyes so he could not only hear but also see the depth of the emotions I could no longer hide from him.

He growled, narrowing his eyes with a smoldering gaze as he lowered his face to mine. His lips crashed against mine, and I replied reverently, eager and desperate to show him. I wanted to prove it with my lips under his, yielding to his demand for more ardor in return. I wanted to demonstrate it with my fingers threaded through his wet hair, gripping for purchase as I worried I'd drown in lust.

He tore back, breaking the kiss with a heaving, hard inhale. "Say it again.

"I love you."

His growl was louder, filthier, like my words were his undoing. Admitting that I wanted him with all my heart was all it took to unleash the beast.

He picked me up, sliding all of our wet skin together in a hot friction of contact. I clung to his neck, mindful of his injuries over his shoulder. In an airborne moment of weightlessness, I spun in his embrace.

Then gasped.

The cold tiles of the shower chilled me, jarring me from the racing pace of the lust that bound us together in here. This intimacy wouldn't abate. He distracted me from the shock of the cool wall at my back as he pushed me up higher against it.

I wrapped my legs around his waist, seeking something to lean against so I wouldn't fall. He lifted me until my breasts were within reach, and he closed his mouth around my nipple. Sucking in my flesh, he teased and tormented me with the ravenous appetite he always had for me. Never idle. Never slow. Alek wanted me, now and always, and knowing I had that pull, that power over him, made me even wetter.

"I love you," I repeated, meaning each syllable as he switched to my other breast and administered the same agonizing pressure of sucks, nips, and licks.

I kept my fingers threaded in his hair as he gave up with a growl. Gathered back into his arms, he moved me again. His aim was the low bench at the back of the generously sized shower stall. The tiles spanned from wall to wall, and once my ass smacked down on the seat built into the opposite end, I shivered.

Between the hot look in his eyes and the cooler contact of my butt on the bench, I was energized and alive. All with the end goal of pleasing my man. As he lowered his head, draping my thighs over his shoulders, I understood the name of this game. I'd please him by letting him turn me to a molten puddle of desire. I'd satisfy him by opening up wide so he could feast on me until I screamed his name.

He didn't wait, dipping his mouth to my pussy and assaulting my sensitive flesh. He slurped and sucked, in a hurry to drag his tongue over me from my taint to my clit. Not one spot went missed, and he doubled back, again and again, to lick up all the cream that dripped so freely from my aching, throbbing, and needy pussy.

I needed him to push me to those heights of bliss. I wanted him to growl and grunt, eating at me like the hungry monster he was.

Modesty was a joke. I relished every filthy, primal, and carnal manner he took me in.

STOLEN BY THE BRATVA

"Please, Alek." I slipped my fingers through his hair again and twisted the dark locks until he hissed. I was a quick learner. I realized yesterday that he enjoyed a bite of pain. And it worked again now. He smashed his face to my pussy as I ground up against his face, humping him to get there faster. My enthusiasm fueled him on, and with a wicked nip at my clit, I screeched out at the sharp hit of tension. My body was alive, burning with the need to come apart under his mouth, but he wasn't ready to end his fun.

"Tell me," he demanded, reaching beneath me as he kneeled closer to the bench. My ass cheeks filled his hands, and as he squeezed hard, digging his fingers into my skin, he thrust his tongue into my pussy faster.

"Fucking tell me, Mila."

"I love—" I choked on my words, overwhelmed with the blinding pressure of coming. I was right there, so close that I'd cry if he stopped again.

"Tell me!"

"I love you," I sobbed as he sucked a stubborn rhythm on my clit. The tension snapped within me, and as waves of pure bliss and relief coursed through me, tingling my every nerve, he hoisted me into his arms.

"I... I..." I couldn't speak, let alone think. All I could do was feel every wave of my orgasm as it knocked me to speechless wonder, each hard inch of his strong body as he held me in his arms and carried me out of the shower.

"I fucking love you too," he growled before kissing me hard.

I hadn't said it to hear it in reply. But now that he'd uttered it, now that he'd shared the reciprocal miracle of loving me back, I was even more overwhelmed with this sweeping euphoria of the orgasm he'd given me.

Reaching up, I closed my lips over his and kissed him hard. I tasted myself on his tongue, and it only made the connection steaming and sizzling between us that much hotter.

We landed on the bed together, soaking wet and slippery from the shower.

He rolled until he covered me, bracing his weight over me while sparing his wounded shoulder. As he stared down at me with a soulful look of possessive pride, I reached up to frame his face.

"I am yours, Alek."

His lips crashed against mine as he lined himself to my pussy.

"I trust you. With my life."

He pushed in his fat cockhead.

"With my body."

"Yes," he agreed, sliding into me with one hard, long thrust.

I caught my breath, reveling in the delicious burn of him stretching me, filling me, and spreading me so fast and hard.

"I want to be yours in every way," I promised, so committed to making him understand the depth and extremes of my submission. Understanding how much this man meant to me was a hard-fought lesson, something I was too stubborn to open my eyes to for so many days. We hadn't been together long to stumble our way to this compromise, but we'd reached this point, nonetheless, a fast fall to complete affection and admiration, and it would never, ever fade or die out between us.

So long as we lived.

"My wife," he said between grunts and breathing hard with his fast thrusts. "My lover," he added, lifting my leg to hold it up so he could pound into me with more force.

"Yes!" I panted, needing that sweet release he pushed me toward.

"And my partner." He paired that final demand, that ultimate declaration, with a deeper spear piercing so deep inside me. I clenched around him, crying out with the force and intensity of the climax he'd summoned. I milked him as he thrust once, twice, and three more times until he jerked and twitched, spilling his hot cum deep into me.

He collapsed over me, pinning me to the bed with his weight. By the time I wrapped my legs around his waist and hugged my arms around his back, he'd slipped and shifted us onto our sides. It still wasn't enough.

He slumped onto his back, his broad chest heaving with the exertion of catching his breath. Still holding me, he tugged me over so I lay at his side, my leg draped over his, my arm on his stomach.

His dick slipped out, smearing our combined juices along my thigh. We were sticky, still soaking wet from the shower, and dampening the bed, but it didn't matter. We lay there together, worn out from both the rush to make love and the weight of admitting our feelings at last.

It wasn't conventional, confessing love after we'd shared our hasty *I dos*. But in our world, with arranged marriages that bound couples together for the sake of duty and tradition, finding love was a rare blessing not many could ever dream to experience.

He stroked his hand over my upper arm, caressing me as I came down from the heady rush of two orgasms. Before that, the ups and downs of the day and night would have been enough to exhaust me.

Now, though, I was alert and at peace. I was where I belonged, with my man. My husband. My ruler. Because it was so much clearer. His mission to clear out the old ways of his bratva. His dedication to get to the bottom of this setup.

I scooched closer, rested my chin on my hand that lay on his chest.

He sighed, moving his free arm behind his head to use it as a pillow. Staring down at me, he arched one brow in question. "Hmm?"

"I have an idea."

He raised his other brow.

"The shipment. It's tomorrow."

He nodded. "I realized it before I got word that Geoff had broken in here."

I blinked, stunned. Here I thought I was being the bigger person, coming clean and rambling *everything* he might want to know. And he'd already been aware.

"You knew the cop was involved?"

He nodded.

I refused to think I had told him all that for nothing. Of course, he would already know. He wasn't dumb.

"If I could get a laptop and log in to my old emails, all those stupid correspondences he had me forwarding to ensure there was no easy route of information being shared…"

He brushed my hair back, smiling slowly. "Yes?"

"Maybe *you* could make sense of the codes and see if there is anything else that would help you prevent my father from trying to bring down your Family."

He dragged me up over his chest to kiss me soundly. "*Our* Family."

I nestled my cheek against his, nuzzling his face. "So you can rule at the top."

"With you at my side, with your unwavering support."

I sighed, rubbing my hand over his chest and feeling the strong thump of his heart, beating in sync with mine, now and forever.

We lay there, committed to being a team for a few more moments until he playfully smacked my ass, prompting me to lift off him and let him get up.

"A laptop, you say?" He grabbed a robe draped on a chair and tossed it to me.

"Yes. I memorized all the log-in details."

He grinned. "Good girl."

I caught the robe, smiling as I shoved my arms through the sleeves and followed him out of the bedroom. He tucked a towel around his waist then grabbed my hand. He held it as he led me to the living room, calling his brother on his cell for him to bring a computer over.

After all the trials and hardships of finding each other, the moment had come to truly work together for our future.

29

ALEK

Morning came quickly, and I woke with a fierce excitement for how the day would likely end. With Mila's help, there was no doubt in my mind that we'd altered the details of the shipment due this afternoon.

I hadn't planned to ask her about any details because I assumed she wouldn't be privy to knowing any. And she hadn't. Her father expected her to mess around with busywork, but with the codes and secrecy, she'd never been able to follow any of it. She hadn't tried to, either, smart enough to know better.

With Nik and Maxim staying over late and picking at *all* the emails she'd fielded at that office, we could piece together enough of what was expected to happen at the Colver dock that we could change up the details of the sting. The DEA was expected to arrive too late, but changing the arrival documentation meant they'd be *early*, just in time to see the Kastavas get caught, not the Valkovs.

Mila agreed with me that she shouldn't sneak near her father's prized dock area. She trusted me to keep her safe, but she understood that Ivan would be a reliable bodyguard in the interim.

STOLEN BY THE BRATVA

I wouldn't have missed this opportunity for the world. I wanted to be there, hiding in the distance and watching in real time as the Kastavas were fucked with this arms shipment coming in.

Sergei Kastava wouldn't have a clue what hit him, and I waited with giddy anticipation as the time crept closer to when the trap would spring.

Instead of accompanying me, Mila went to the shops to begin building a wardrobe fit for a woman in her position. At the top of the Valkov Bratva, she had to dress the part. She'd look good in anything. I already knew she had an eye for fashion and was practiced in accentuating her looks. All I cared to find out was what she purchased for me. Her lingerie would still be *hers*, but really, it was a treat for me, too. I couldn't wait to uncover and unwrap her and see her in naughty, teasing lingerie in bed.

Ivan would keep her safe. I trusted my brother without a doubt. In fact, I counted on all the men who'd heeded my orders under Pavel's leadership. I'd instructed every Valkov man to make himself scarce as the hour drew near. I wanted no one but the die-hard loyalists to my uncle to be here and caught.

The moment came, and with a swarm of activity, detectives, agents, and officers filled the dockyard. Kastava soldiers tried to run or open fire. The thugs on the ship fired as well, and a small war had broken out as the law enforcement agencies came down hard on the bratva men who hadn't learned of Mila's and my plan to thwart them.

I remained back in the shadows with Nikolai. We watched it all come crashing down, and at the end, we shared a knowing look and smile.

"You did it," he congratulated me.

"*We* did it." All my suspicions had paid off. From the beginning, I knew this shipment and supposed alliance with the Kastava Family would end in ruin. And it had. I'd helped to bring it all down, and I was walking away from the mess with a wife and a clear drive to lead instead of my uncle.

"You sure you don't want help this afternoon?" he asked as we strolled away, heading for our cars.

I shook my head. "I already have my help lined up. Thanks."

"Sure thing, *Boss*." He smirked, clearly excited for this new path we were forging for the future.

I smiled, confident but not cocky.

As we'd planned, I drove to Pavel's mansion. It had once been the home that my grandparents had lived in, and soon enough, it would be filled with a family unit again. Whores and gamblers wouldn't hang out in the parlor and overstay their welcome anymore. Drunk soldiers wouldn't break dishes in the kitchen. Pavel wouldn't stain the furniture and waste away the fine heirlooms that had been in the house for generations.

Change was coming, and it would start here, in my uncle's office. Mila and Ivan arrived just after I did.

"How much?"

"Damage?" Ivan asked with a smirk.

Mila rolled her eyes at him. "Hush."

Ivan smiled and nodded at me on his way out.

"How much?" I asked again, curious whether Mila even knew.

She listed a number, and I was impressed.

"What?" she asked as I sat in my uncle's chair behind the antique desk that should have been my father's. I rubbed my hand over the smooth, polished wood.

"I just wanted to know if you even knew what you spent."

She nodded. "Until we can improve the Family's businesses, I don't need to be wasting money for no good reason."

As if I needed another reason to love you more. She wasn't a materialistic woman. I'd already guessed that much. She cared about deeper, more lasting things like love and freedom. She wasn't like other women, careless about their spending and oblivious to details. Of course, she paid attention. She was diligent and was always conscientious about her actions in everything she did. My wife wasn't a frivolous person.

She sat on my lap when I beckoned her closer. She'd arrived with Ivan right after I'd found my mother's ring, and with her seated on my thigh, I took her hand and slipped it on.

"This—" She huffed a laugh. "I *just* told you that I don't need riches and wealth. How much did you spend on *this*?"

I kissed her finger just below where I'd placed the diamonds. "Not a thing. It was my mother's. I found it here, deep in a drawer of the desk."

"He took it?" she asked, scowling at what else my uncle had done.

"Among so much more," I replied bitterly before the man himself entered the room.

"What—" He sneered at us, locking his eyes on my wife. "What the fuck is that Kastava scum doing here?"

Then he turned his wrath to me, flustered and turning red in the face. "Explain yourself!" He flailed his fists, enraged and near exploding with the force of his anger. "First, I show up to that alliance that fell apart because of *your* actions—"

"You mean the coup my father tried to pull on you?" Mila sassed.

He blustered, opening and closing his mouth like a fish out of water.

"Then you kill my son!" He smacked his fist to his chest. "The heir to the bratva!"

I would take it to the grave that the magnificent woman on my lap was my cousin's killer.

I shook my head. "You're looking at him." I tossed the birth certificates to the desktop. "You set my father up so you could kill him. Because Pyotr Valkov was the firstborn twin. He was the rightful Pakhan, and you killed him to have the power for yourself."

"That's bullshit!" he roared, reaching for the gun he never bothered to actually wear anymore.

"It was. And it's time for a new future for the family." I lifted the gun I'd rested on the desktop. "I'm the rightful heir, the rightful leader, and with my wife, *we* will lead the Valkov Bratva to its former glory and might."

I aimed and shot only once, sinking a bullet right between his eyes.

His mouth remained open in an O of surprise. Mila barely flinched. She stayed cool and collected as she sat on my lap, and together, we watched him drop to the floor. Within moments of his fall, Ivan and a couple of other soldiers came in to remove his body. After they'd taken him out, silence filled the office.

Peace and hope did as well, and as I felt Mila sigh and relax against me, I knew this was only the beginning.

Of my rule. Of my real Family. Right here, with the daughter of my enemy.

"It's all done now," she murmured, rubbing her hand along my jawline.

I gazed at her, letting her see all the love and commitment that I could offer her. With a slow smile, I shook my head. "As far as I'm concerned, my life can only truly begin now."

She bit her lip and leaned closer to kiss me, promising my prediction with the impatience to make that come true.

30

MILA

wo months later...

"All I'm saying is that it would make more sense if we handled the wallpaper first, *then* ordered new furniture." I set my hands on my hips and raised my brows at my brothers-in-law.

Of all the things that I needed to adjust to, remembering that I had a family was the biggest change. Brothers, soldiers who acted like brothers, loyal men who served Alek like he'd belonged as their Pakhan all this time. I had a support team. I no longer had my father. I'd cut him out of my mind and heart since I moved into the Valkov mansion with my husband. I would never cease to wonder at the inclusivity of these men, and slowly but surely, introducing more women to this family would be a blessing.

I tilted my head to the side, considering Ivan and Maxim. *Which of you should be the first to work on that, hmm?*

Nikolai entered the room, carrying more boxes. He furrowed his brows at the way I studied his brothers. "Why's she looking at you like that?"

ı, never mind me. Just mentally getting excited to play matchmaker for all of you one day.

Nik narrowed his eyes at Ivan. "You're not talking crap around her, are you?"

Ivan smirked. "She's got a dirtier mouth than anyone else around here."

"Wallpaper?" Maxim said with a wince as he eyed the room. "I don't know anything about wallpaper."

Nikolai groaned, setting the boxes down and holding his hands up in a truce as he backed away. "No. Don't look at me. I'm not getting involved with redecorating."

Ivan edged out of the room through the other door. "Just tell Alek!"

Maxim nodded. "He'll just hire a crew."

I rolled my eyes. "Oh, come on."

He grimaced and shook his head. "I'm all for helping you move stuff out and making room for you to, well, make this place feel like a home again, but wallpapering is a whole other thing." He mimicked his brother, holding his hands up in a truce as he left me giggling there.

I wasn't seriously going to ask them to personally handle this room's renovation. Still, I wasn't wounded by their bailing from the topic. Each time I chatted with Alek's brothers, I got to know them a little better.

For the first time in all my life, I was looking forward to the future with a deep sense of unshakable excitement. In this house, with this family, I would never be bartered or taken for granted again. I was part of an honest-to-God family here, and I would never be an object to discard ever again.

My place was right at Alek's side, and after I checked the time, I left this room to find him. He'd be done with his workout about now, and

I was too excited to wait for him to shower and clean up to talk to him.

It seemed my estimate of time was off. I found him in our bedroom, already showered. He exited the bathroom, still with a towel around his waist, and just that look had my lust skyrocketing.

Upon seeing me there, he grinned and dropped the terrycloth. "Well, hello there, Wife," he drawled sexily.

I hummed my appreciation, reaching out to stroke his cock as he stalked toward me. He angled me back on the bed as I traced his long shaft, but I stalled, playing hard to get as he pushed up my sundress.

"Alek, we're far too busy for that now."

He growled, tipping me back on the bed and dragging my panties off. "That's crazy talk."

I giggled, trying to slip out of his reach, but he was faster. He always was. The chase was part of the fun, but with my current mood, I gave in to his sliding his dick into me.

"Ooohhhh..." I moaned, kissing him as he started to thrust into me slowly.

"Too busy, huh?"

I nodded. "Even for a quickie."

He scoffed, pounding into me harder, just the way I liked it.

"We've got designers coming in soon to redecorate the office." Neither of us wanted Pavel's influence to linger in there. "You've got a meeting soon."

"Shh." He lowered to kiss me quiet.

"And I want to speak to the chef again."

He furrowed his brows. "You're talking about another man while your husband fucks you?"

I ignored his teasing. I knew he wasn't mad. He knew that I loved and wanted him, only him. "It's going to feel like a real family around here, Alek." I lost my roll, moaning at his dick filling me so well. "Starting with the big dinner tonight with all your closest men."

He smiled, laughing once as he fucked me. "A big dinner? Why so formal?"

"To celebrate."

He growled, fucking me faster. "We're celebrating right now."

I whimpered, grabbing him to kiss him sweetly.

"I love whatever you plan, Mila. I love *you*. Only you. Forever."

Just before my orgasm could hit and rob me of speech, I smiled. "Will you have room in your heart for our child as well?"

He slowed, then stopped deep inside me as he went speechless. A look of shocked wonder crossed his face, and he resumed fucking me harder, thrilled.

"I'll love our children." He growled as I clenched around him, panting as the waves of my orgasm coursed through me with sweet relief. "Of course, I will love them."

"Even if it's not a boy?" I asked, worried. Men and their sons would always be more important in our world.

He laughed, tensing as he came and filled me. "I *want* a girl first. A spitfire, just like her mother. Because our past is going to stay in the past, and we've got a hell of a future to build as we go forward now."

I pulled him down for a kiss. "Together."

"Together forever," he agreed.

Printed in Great Britain
by Amazon